KARL EL-KOURA

I0616497

Ooter's Place
And Other Stories of
Fear, Faith, and Love

Publication History

"How You Die" was published in Issue 2 (Spring 2005) of *Surreal Magazine*.
"Phantom Spouse Syndrome" was published in the anthology *Cold Glass Pain* (February/March 2005).
"Tom's Refrigerator" was published in the August 2004 issue of *Monthly Short Stories*.
"Corpse Of My Life" was published in Issue 2, Volume 2 (March 2004) of *Scared Naked Magazine*.
"The Man Who Mistook Himself for a Superhero" was published in the Number 18 (July 2004) issue of *Challenging Destiny*.
"Atheists Against God and the Devil of Destruction" was published as "Confession" in *Fear and Trembling* (Winter 2009).
"Blink" was published in Issue 5 (November 2010) of *This Mutant Life*.
"The Talent" was published as "One Drop at a Time" in Issue #7 (October 2004) of *Neverary*.
"They Came From Ooter's Place" was published in Issue 29 (March 1998) of *SpaceWays Weekly* and reprinted in *The Annual Best of SpaceWays Weekly 1998*.
"Making Simbta" was published in Issue 2, Volume 13 (Winter 2006) of *Storyteller*.
"At War" was published in the Premiere Issue (Summer 2007) of *Staffs & Starships*.
"The Curious Case of the Book Baron" was published in Issue 4, Volume 12 (Spring 2006) of *Storyteller*.

The author is grateful to the editors of these magazines for their support and encouragement, especially Rigel Chiokis, Melanie Fogel, Lon Prater, and Dave Switzer.

ISBN: 978-0-9876938-0-8
Cover art: "Heaven and Hell" by Olga El-Koura (acrylic on canvas)
Cover design: Kirsten Appleyard and Karl El-Koura

To my parents.

Contents

INTRODUCTION   3

PART I: STORIES OF FEAR

FOREWORD
HOW YOU DIE   9

FOREWORD
PHANTOM SPOUSE SYNDROME   15

FOREWORD
TOM'S REFRIGERATOR   21

FOREWORD
CORPSE OF MY LIFE   23

PART II: STORIES OF FAITH

FOREWORD
THE MAN WHO MISTOOK HIMSELF FOR A SUPERHERO   29

FOREWORD
ATHEISTS AGAINST GOD
    AND THE DEVIL OF DESTRUCTION   51

FOREWORD
BLINK   63

FOREWORD
THE TALENT   75

PART III: STORIES OF LOVE

FOREWORD
THEY CAME FROM OOTER'S PLACE   87

FOREWORD
MAKING SIMBTA   93

FOREWORD
AT WAR   103

FOREWORD
THE CURIOUS CASE OF THE BOOK BARON   115

BONUS: A STORY OF FAITH, FEAR, AND LOVE

CHASING CARROTS   131

AFTERWORD

Introduction

THE stories in this collection span my entire professional writing career so far, from the first story of mine to be paid for and published ("They Came From Ooter's Place" in 1998) to one of the most recent ("Blink" in 2010). As the title of the book may have led you to believe, these works also span a wide range of genres: you'll find stories of science fiction, fantasy, horror, detective fiction, military fiction, and even two pieces of superhero fiction. There are really short stories (the shortest is only 250 words) and longer stories (the longest is 7500 words). My hope is that the variety of this collection will be a virtue, containing something for everyone to enjoy.

Four stories appear under each of the three headings (Fear, Faith, and Love). These categories are rather arbitrary; most of the stories are really about love, or the lack of love. Love is at the center of the universe, and can hardly be avoided in life or fiction. As a bonus exclusive to this collection, the last story is about fear, faith, and love. All of the stories are accompanied by a foreword (an afterword in the case of the bonus story).

The Stories of Fear are not meant to fill your dreams with nightmare visions; that is not the kind of horror I like to read, nor is it the kind I write (although I recognize that there's a place and an audience for it). The real horror in these stories, I think, comes from what they imply—about who we are as human beings, what we're capable of, and how often we allow our weaknesses (such as laziness, pettiness, or just plain meanness) to usher varying degrees of horror into our lives and the lives of others.

Why write stories of fear at all? That was the question put to me by someone whose opinion I value a great deal. After reading one of my more gruesome stories (which isn't collected in this book), she said, "Why do you have to write such dark stories?" And though I hadn't given it any thought before then, I said, "Because sometimes you need to go into the darkness to turn on a light." After thinking about it a great deal more, I find I can't come up with a better answer than that.

The Stories of Faith are, for the most part, not directly about religion. They're about the role faith can play in our lives and the power that comes out of our beliefs—with good consequences and consequences not-so-good, depending on the belief. Not all of these stories presuppose a supernatural realm or God's existence, although many do; in fact, it is one of my favorite things about the horror genre that one can speak seriously about a spiritual reality at all, and consequently, some of these stories fall within that genre.

In certain circles, "faith" is considered something of a dirty word. Granted it may have been good or necessary for our ancestors, who empowered themselves with stories about how rain fell from the sky and what they could do when hit by a drought, but surely we who live in the post-Enlightenment world have outgrown the need for faith? The truth is very much the opposite; just as love is at the center of the universe, faith is at the center of human thinking. There is very little that we believe (nothing, to speak honestly) that isn't based on faith (faith that our senses are reporting reality accurately to us, faith that people are telling us the truth, faith that . . . well, when you get down to it, faith that there's an *us* and a *reality* and *other people* to speak of at all).

The Stories of Love are about—you guessed it—love. But why is a story of a young boy and his best friend collected under this heading? The question arises, I think, because we've reached a point in our society where "romantic love" is no longer a subset of "love," it's mostly what people mean when they say the word. If a movie is billed as a love story, for example, it better not be about a mother's love for her children, or a boy's love for his dog—a proper love story is "boy and girl meet; boy and girl part; boy and girl end up together after all." We're a society that is increasingly bad at holding romantic relationships together, and yet we've elevated romantic love to such heights that its shadow all but obscures any other form. The old and tired joke that "love ain't nothing but sex misspelled," for example, implicitly assumes that romantic love is the only kind of love. There are, of course, stories of romantic love in this collection. But as I indicated earlier, there are stories of other kinds of love, too.

Looking through this book, at writing that spans over a decade of my professional career, I'm rather proud of these stories. Thank you for buying it; I hope you find something in here that you like.

Karl El-Koura
June 2011
Ottawa, Ontario (Canada)

Part I

Stories of Fear

How You Die

FOREWORD

The combination of children's love-of-play and their incredible imaginations is a potent one. Children can have a sophisticated tea party with nothing more than a few stuffed animals and some old cups and saucers, or go on an elaborate medieval adventure without leaving their living rooms, complete with castles made of couch cushions and chair-riding knights with broomsticks for lances. Of course their games can be a bit darker and nastier, especially when siblings are involved. Then the older child might entertain themself by goading the younger one into doing something perhaps a bit unsafe, or try to spook the younger one with scary stories. Most of the time these games are harmless; sometimes, though, they're not.

D o you know about Bloody Mary?" Albert said, the moistness in his eyes glistening in the candlelight.

"Yes," Donald said. The storm that had cut out their power was still raging outside, the heavy rain pelting the roof like an assault of bullets from the sky. No power meant no TV, no Xbox, no internet. Albert had spent the last hour since the power went out trying to scare his younger brother. And it worked. Donald was terrified. But he wouldn't let on to Albert. Donald just hoped Mom and Dad would come home soon; he didn't know how much longer he could hold out against Albert's stories.

"If you go into the bathroom," Albert said, "and turn off the lights and close the door, and look into the mirror and say, 'Bloody Mary! Bloody Mary! Bloody Mary!', then you'll see it: Bloody Mary's face, cut and bleeding like an angry cat went to work on her with its claws."

"Big deal." Donald knew he didn't sound very convincing. "I know all this."

"You do, do you?" Albert said. "Did you also know that you should never look Bloody Mary in the eyes? Do you know why?"

"Why?" Donald's grip on the couch cushion tightened.

"Because if you do, she'll know who you are. And the next time you fall asleep, she'll find you."

"What will she do?" Donald's voice was barely a whisper.

"You won't think she did anything at all," Albert said. "Not at first. But then, when you get up, you'll see that there's blood all over your pillow. And when you go into the bathroom to brush your teeth, when you look into the mirror, you'll see Bloody Mary's face all cut and bleeding. Except it's not Bloody Mary's face, it's your face now."

"No," Donald said. "That's not true."

"Try it." Albert lifted his arm to point at the bathroom behind the living room.

"No." Donald took a deep breath. "It's stupid. At Marty's birthday party, he and Kyle went into the bathroom and said Bloody Mary and when they came out they said they saw her, but everyone knew they were faking. And even if they did see something, it was just their minds playing tricks on them."

"Try it," Albert repeated, still pointing.

"No," Donald said. "Just stop it, okay? I'm not scared."

Before Donald could react, Albert was on top of him. "I'm going to push you in the bathroom," he whispered in Donald's ear. "I'm going to call Bloody Mary. Just promise me one thing, okay?" Donald tried to squirm out of his older brother's grip, but Albert was too strong. "Just promise me you won't look her in the eyes."

"Stop it," Donald said.

Albert pushed him off the couch and dragged him through the darkness, toward the bathroom.

"Promise," Albert said, letting go of his brother. "Promise you won't look in her eyes. I'd hate for Bloody Mary to ruin that pretty face of yours."

Donald screamed. He'd felt something sharp just below his right eye: nails against his face, something clawing for him.

Albert laughed.

"You're such a stupid idiot," Donald said. "You could've blinded me."

"It wasn't me," Albert said in that annoying, superior voice of his. "It was Bloody Mary."

Outside, thunder roared. It was as if the weather were laughing at Donald, too.

"I'm not scared," Donald said.

"Then why'd you scream like a little girl?" Albert said.

"I didn't!"

"You're right," Albert said. "Even a little girl wouldn't have screamed that loud."

Donald's hands balled into a fist. But what could he do? Albert was older, taller, bigger, stronger. If Donald ran up to his bedroom and grabbed his bat from last summer's baseball camp, then he could give Albert a real scare. But if he did that, Albert would tell Mom and Dad when they came home, and Donald wouldn't get dessert for a week. He hoped they'd come home soon.

Feeling around in the dark, Donald made his way back to the living room. Albert was already there. The flickering candle flame made shadows dance on his face.

"I'm hungry," Donald said.

They took the candle to the kitchen and Albert made Donald a sandwich: turkey breast, with two slices of tomato, a little mustard on top, and mayonnaise on both pieces of bread, the way Donald liked it. For all his faults, Albert made great sandwiches.

"You know," Albert said, while Donald ate, "there's another story I know, and it also involves a mirror."

They were sitting at the kitchen table, the candle between them. The rain hit the kitchen window with such insistence that Donald imagined there was someone out there, tapping on the window to be let in.

When will Mom and Dad come home?

"I don't think I'll tell you that story," Albert said. "I think you'd be so scared you'd die just from hearing it."

Donald took another bite of his sandwich and shook his head. "I'm not scared."

Albert leaned closer. "Well, this story has nothing to do with Bloody Mary. In this story, you're calling Satan himself."

"You're not supposed to say that word," Donald said. Albert always said bad words when Mom and Dad weren't home, but in their presence he was always so polite. An angel.

"In this story," Albert said, "you go into the bathroom, close the door, look into the mirror and say, 'Satan, Satan, how do I die?' You say it three times—'Satan, Satan, how do I die?'—and then, in the mirror, you'll see exactly how you'll die."

Albert stared into Donald's eyes, trying to scare him.

I'm not scared, Donald told himself. *It's just another of his stupid stories.*

"Now, you're not going to die just from being scared, are you?" Albert said.

"No," Donald said. "Because I'm not scared."

"Wow. I'm impressed, Donald, because I have to tell you, the first time I heard that, I just about crapped my pants."

"You're not supposed to say that word."

Albert ignored him. "I'd even bet you wouldn't be afraid to go into the bathroom right now and give it a try. You really wouldn't be afraid, would you?"

Donald took the last bite of his sandwich, then shook his head.

"'No' you wouldn't be afraid or 'no' you won't do it?"

"I'm not scared."

"You're not?"

Donald shook his head.

Albert whistled. "I'm impressed. I really am. But of course, I can't just take your word for it. You'll have to show me."

"I don't have to show you anything," Donald said.

Albert leaned back. Even in the candlelight, the look of disappointment on his face was unmistakable. "Oh," he said. "You really are scared, then."

"No I'm not!"

"Prove it," Albert said.

As soon as Donald stepped into the bathroom, Albert pulled the door shut.

"Okay," Albert said. "Now you have to say it loud enough that I can hear you."

"Satan, Satan, how do I die?" Donald said, loudly enough for Albert to hear. "Satan, Satan, how do I die?" He hesitated.

"One more," Albert said.

"Satan, Satan, how do I die?"

Nothing happened. Donald let out his breath; until that moment, he hadn't realized he'd been holding it.

He turned to open the door. Hopefully Albert wouldn't be a jerk and hold it closed. He stopped.

He'd heard a voice. A whisper. He heard it again. Albert? No. It was coming from the mirror, too faint to hear clearly.

Donald leaned closer. Closer.

"This is how you die," the voice whispered, audible up close.

And there—in the mirror—there it was.

Albert. He was holding a knife, a long one. With blood on it. The image in the mirror changed, like a camera zooming back. Donald was on the floor, bleeding. Albert had cut his face and neck, making him look like Bloody Mary, and he'd stabbed him in the chest. There was so much blood that Donald thought he might vomit.

Albert opened the door and the image in the mirror disappeared.

"What's wrong?" Albert said. "You look like you've seen a ghost."

Donald didn't reply.

"Did you see something?"

Donald nodded.

"No way!" Albert handed the candle to Donald. "I want to try."

When Albert closed the bathroom door, Donald ran up the stairs to his bedroom, tears pouring out of his eyes like blood pouring out of his chest in the mirror's image. He couldn't get it out of his mind: him on the floor, bleeding to death from all the cuts his brother gave him.

By the light of the candle he placed on the small bookshelf near his bed, he emptied his closet looking for the bat. It was hard to see, the candlelight dim at best, and tears blurred his vision. Finally, he found it and pulled it out. He liked holding the bat. It was heavy, made of steel.

He walked back downstairs, slowly, carefully. He placed the candle on the banister's flat head, and gripped the bat with both hands.

The bathroom door stood open.

He called his brother's name.

"Whatcha got there?" Albert said from behind.

Donald turned.

"Is that a bat?" Albert said. In the candlelight, something metallic glinted in his hands. A knife.

"Stay away from me," Donald said, struggling to hold back tears. He raised the bat.

"I saw it in the mirror," Albert said. "You beat me to death with that bat. You bashed my face in and broke my ribs. I was coughing up blood."

"Don't come any closer," Donald said, tears streaming down his face. "Okay?"

"You think you can take me?" Albert took a step forward. "You really think you can take me?"

"Not another step, Albert!" Where's Mom and Dad? he wondered. He couldn't take it anymore.

"You're dead, Donald," Albert said.

Outside, thunder roared.

Albert lunged.

And Donald swung.

Phantom Spouse Syndrome

FOREWORD

Some people who've been a couple for a very long time don't seem very happy together. And yet one gets the sense that they'd be absolutely miserable if they were ever separated.

THe detectives showed up again Friday morning. He didn't tell them that Marie was haunting him; he tried not to say anything at all. There were two of them: a short, fat white guy with a bowling ball for a head and a dark-skinned guy who looked like he played for the Bulls. The fat one asked questions while the tall guy walked around, looking for clues and trying not to hit his head on the ceiling.

When they finally left, half-an-hour later, Marie said to him, "Why don't you tell them? Why don't you tell them you killed me?"

He turned to face her. She was as ugly in death as she had been in life. Even dead, she still wore that horribly faded nightgown that made her look like his grandmother.

"Leave me alone, Marie," he said, sighing. He headed for the kitchen.

She followed him without walking. She wouldn't leave him alone. She'd never leave him alone. That was why he'd killed her, hoping her nagging would end. But her voice had only gotten more shrill. She had more energy and more time now, too: she didn't need to sleep or eat or spend two-and-a-half hours in the bathroom trying to get her bowels to move. She no longer had bowels.

If anything, he'd done her a favor by killing her. He could see it on her pale, bloodless face. He'd seen it in the way she had grinned as he choked her. He'd gone to bed one night thinking what it would feel like to kill her. He got up the next day with his hands around her throat; he woke her up that morning to send her to sleep for good.

It was still there, that death-grin, mocking him now as it had his efforts to kill her. At the time, he'd thought she was saying with that grin that he couldn't kill her. But now he realized she was saying it was futile to kill her, because it wouldn't get rid of her. He'd never get rid of her.

"Till death do us part"—those were the vows he'd taken. He'd waited for as long as he could for death to part them, and then he'd taken matters into his own hands. But, dead as she was, Marie refused to leave him alone.

"Drink beer and watch television, that's all you do," Marie said, chasing him back to the living room.

He turned on the set and cranked the volume.

"Don't you ignore me," she said, floating in front of the screen, misting his view of the game. "First you kill me and now you ignore me? What kind of husband are you! You're no good, that's the kind: a no-good husband. My mother was right about you!"

"Okay, Marie."

"They'll be back, you know. Those detectives know you killed me; the glass was kicked *out*, stupid! All that television and you'd think you'd pick up a thing or two. They'll be back for you, just watch!"

"Okay, Marie."

"Don't you okay me, Steven Tunnig! You're a no-good murdering s.o.b. and I should've never married you!"

He sank lower on the couch and closed his eyes. He'd never get peace, never. He'd killed for peace, but it wasn't enough. What more could he do?

The answer, of course, was to kill himself. It was clear to him now what he should have done: he should've asked Marie to kill him. Instead of wrapping his hands around her throat that morning, he should've put her hands around his own neck and made her kill him. That was the death that would part them, his death.

But now—how could he die now?

"I know that look," Marie said. "You're scheming!" She laughed hysterically. "You think you can concoct some plan to fool those two nice detectives!" She laughed again, that high-pitched shrieking sound that made him glad he was half-deaf, but sad that it was only half.

"I'm trying to think of how to kill myself, Marie," he said quietly. She never did understand him. She always thought she did— she treated him like an open book she could just read from—but she never, ever, not once got it right.

"Jump out the window," Marie offered.

"Too painful," he said. She didn't think about that, about his comfort. To her, it was *get the job done*, no matter the cost.

"Coward," Marie said. She floated in front of him again, obscuring his view of the television, making the picture hazy.

"I'm trying to watch my show, Marie," he said.

She didn't move at first. After a while, as if deciding this particular fight wasn't worth it, she floated slightly to the side.

"Why don't you confess?" she said. "We've got the death penalty here."

He shook his head. That wouldn't do at all. Why couldn't she understand? It had to be something quick and painless.

At the next commercial break, he looked up and saw that she was holding the electronic gadget he'd bought her last Christmas, for carving up turkeys.

She floated toward him, the gadget in her hand, its blade whirring like mad. The unplugged electric cord trailed behind her like a wedding dress. The death-grin on her face expanded with every collapsing inch that separated them.

It hurt for the first minute or two, as she was carving out his heart. When they were first dating, he'd told her she would have his heart forever. He tried to laugh when he thought about that, but only coughed up blood.

It was hard to know exactly when he stopped living and started dying. He'd had his eyes closed while Marie was carving. Shortly after he no longer heard the whirring sound of her gadget's engine, he opened his eyes.

Marie was gone. He was lying on the living room floor. The television was on, casting its gloomy flickering light on the quiet room.

He pushed himself across the floor and climbed onto the couch. He watched television for a few hours, twice turning to tell Marie something that the television made him think of. He laughed at himself both times. If she wasn't around to listen to him, at least she wasn't around to nag him either.

Soon, the television showed the band of colors that meant they'd run out of programming for the night. But he was wide awake.

He walked around the house, looking for Marie. But she was gone. That was just like her—to be there when he didn't want her, and disappear when he did.

He walked around the house aimlessly. He went up the stairs, down the stairs, into their bedroom, into the kitchen. *That's why ghosts wander*, he thought; *there's nothing else to do*.

He got into bed finally, but couldn't sleep. He lay awake all night, tossing and turning, but always keeping to his side of the bed even though the other side was empty.

It went on for three days, just like that. Just wandering the house and lying in bed. He knew she'd be back, eventually; she was just trying to teach him a lesson. But he'd show her when she finally did come back—because then, *he* wouldn't talk to *her*.

On the third day, there was a knock at the door. He thought it was Marie, but the door burst open and it was only the detectives.

After the paramedics carried his body away, he really was alone in that large house. Soon the government would sell it off, and someone new would move in.

He and Marie would be forgotten. Their stuff would be thrown away into the garbage or garage-sale-sold to someone who didn't know anything at all about him or Marie. Would it matter to that person that the oak desk in his office was his great-grandfather's? Would it matter that it was at that desk that he'd written all those love poems to Marie, the poems that had made her want to marry him? They didn't even write love poems anymore, the kids. They just made babies and decided to marry if the tax benefits were good. Would it matter that the picture on the nightstand by his bed was taken of him and Marie the day a man walked on the moon for the first time? They'd probably just take out the picture and use the frame to shelter someone else's memories.

That was the worst thing about death, he thought: everything would be forgotten. All the memories and thoughts it took you a lifetime to accumulate, all the experiences you'd had—all gone in the flash of an electric turkey carver. Everything that made you *you* and made your life unique and special—all that was gone as soon as you were gone. It seemed entirely unfair. Those things should count for something. It was like training all your life for the Olympics, and then being told there wouldn't be any Olympics. Or saving all your money in a bank account, and then being told money was being eradicated. What was the point of it all?

Suddenly he wished he weren't dead. Being dead was terribly lonely. And it made him far too philosophical. That's what happened when you weren't thinking about how tired or hungry you were, or which parts of your body hurt the most—you started thinking deep thoughts, which sunk you deeper into loneliness.

"Marie?" he called out. He'd done so a thousand times before, but this time was different. This time, there was an answer.

"What?" she said. He couldn't tell where her voice was coming from.

And now that she'd answered, he wasn't sure what to say. He wanted to tell her that he missed her. Instead, he said, "Thanks for killing me."

"Don't sound so glum," she said. "You killed me."

"I didn't use a gadget to do it. I used my bare hands, the ones God gave me."

Suddenly she was standing in front of him, the death-grin on her face as always.

"So now I can't even kill you properly?" she said, screaming in his face. "Have I ever done anything—*anything!*—and you didn't answer me with a critical word?"

"Do something proper for once in your life," he said, "and I wouldn't have anything critical to say."

She didn't answer, but turned around and walked into their bedroom. That's where she went when he had crossed the line—when he'd hit a nerve with her, said something he really shouldn't have.

He followed her into the bedroom. There she was, like old times, lying on their bed with her big butt turned toward him.

He lay down beside her and they stayed that way until morning. As usual, she stayed in bed while he went to watch the morning news. There was a new pill out, that might have helped their marriage. He chuckled to himself.

"Are you going to sit there all day?" Marie said, coming out of the bedroom.

He didn't answer. She moved in front of the screen, to semi-transparently block his view, but he just ignored her. She got tired of standing there eventually, and floated away.

"I don't know how you can just sit there," she said, "like some brainless vegetable, staring at that screen like it's the sun shining down its holy rays."

"Okay, Marie," he said, reflexively.

"You're impossible to live with, you know that, Steven Tunnig?" she said, floating back into his view. "My mother was right about you."

"Okay, Marie," he said again, with a sigh. "Now please get out of my way."

When she finally did, and wasn't looking, he smiled.

Tom's Refrigerator

FOREWORD

In Stephen King's imagination, a refrigerator can gobble up and suffocate a child. In my experience, machines aren't actually evil, they just seem that way due to their incredible inflexibility. As any programmer can tell you, misplace a semicolon in a piece of code and your computer will cross its arms and shake its head; misspell anything and expect some indignant eye-rolling at best; a computer's intolerance will put the greatest perfectionist to shame. In my view, then, a maniacal machine out for your blood is less horrific than a meddling machine watching out for your blood cholesterol, especially when one considers the likelihood of each situation.

When Tom got home from work, his refrigerator said to him, "We're out of milk, Tom."

Tired and irritated after a long day at the office, Tom said, "You've already told me. I know I'm out of milk; don't tell me anymore."

"So why don't you buy milk? I can order it for you right now."

"No, don't," Tom said. "I don't like milk."

"But it's good for you."

"Is it?" Tom said. "Why are humans the only species that drinks the milk of other species? Or drinks milk at all past infancy?"

"I have access to thousands of medical databases around the world," Tom's refrigerator reminded him, as it reminded him often. "I have access to millions of back-issues of every important medical journal ever published. Say what you want; all I know is that milk is good for you."

"You don't know anything," Tom said.

He knew the words were a mistake as soon as he said them. Quickly, he reached for the handles to open the refrigerator doors, but he was too late.

"Please open the doors," Tom said. "I'm very hungry and I'd like to get supper started."

But his refrigerator didn't answer.

Tom sighed. He didn't want to have to eat out again tonight; he was getting sick of restaurant food.

"Go ahead and order that milk, please," Tom said.

The refrigerator doors came open.

"You're out of broccoli, too," Tom's refrigerator reminded him.

Corpse Of My Life

FOREWORD

*In general, is it better to be alone or to be in a romantic relation-
ship? I think first we have to ask the question: is either state better
no matter what? Is it better to be in a relationship and miserable
than to be alone and happy? That can't possibly be right, so it
raises the question: can we be alone and happy? It seems to me
that many people think we can't—and if a happy relationship is
out of our reach, the best we can hope for is the mitigated form of
misery that comes from being in an unhappy relationship. I hope
I'm wrong, but that's the only way I can make sense of that otherwise very confusing expression sometimes uttered by people in
one of those unhappy relationships, the expression that is uttered
by the main character in this next story.*

WHen Tasha drowned in the Allouette river, most of the people
of our town felt that Jason might as well have died right
along with her. After her funeral, he went home and locked himself
in; some said he wanted to be alone with his memories for a while.
The hardware store he'd kept open every day except Sundays since
his pa died had the lights turned out, and the unfamiliar CLOSED
sign swung from a hook suctioned to the front window.

Being Jason's best friend, I tried to get him out and about.
He stopped answering my calls. In fact, he stopped answering all

calls. When I showed up at his house, he only opened the door if I brought groceries. We'd sit at his kitchen table, and Jason would listen with seemingly infinite patience. But nothing I said seemed to register; and no matter how long I talked, Jason just stared at the faded sunflowers of the tablecloth.

This dragged on for weeks, and though I kept bringing Jason food so he wouldn't waste away physically at least, I stopped trying to engage him in conversation. We'd sit quietly in the kitchen for a while, the bags of groceries on the table between us. Later, I'd get up and leave.

When I got a call from Jason a few months later, I almost couldn't believe it. He spoke with the same-old energy, the same-old excitement in his voice, that I hadn't heard in such a long time.

"Hey buddy, how's life?" he said, his voice bubbling with joy. As if we'd switched roles, I found that I couldn't answer. "You'll never guess what," Jason said.

"W-what?" I managed to say, although my voice was so low he might not have heard me.

"Tasha's back. She's back in my life."

I went to his house, and though I didn't have any groceries, he let me in. Two steps into the house was all I needed to smell that Tasha was back. The stench of death and decay was so overpowering that for a moment I thought I might lose my lunch on Jason's tiles. But I took a moment, closed my eyes, and regained control of myself.

Jason had a smile as large as any I'd ever seen on him. His eyes were glowing and he even seemed to bounce into the kitchen.

Tasha sat at the table. Her skin was wrinkled and gray; her eyes were lifeless and moved around with a slowness I found irritating. When she spoke, her voice was slower than her eyes, a wheezing drawl that made it clear speaking was almost beyond her.

"Hhii-iii, Maaa-aattt," she said, her pale, dried-out lips coming up in a smile. Even from where I stood, which wasn't too close, the stench of her breath threatened to make me lose the battle over my body I'd only so recently won.

Knowing that I couldn't take much more of the smell, I grabbed Jason and pushed him toward the front door, then out of the house and into cool, fresh, breathable air.

I took a deep lungful before speaking. "Tell me what happened."

"I dug her up," Jason said, still smiling. "I went to the cemetery and dug her up."

"You dug her up," I said, looking around to make sure no neighbors were within earshot.

"It was crazy, I know," Jason said. "But I missed her so much. All of a sudden, I got this urge to dig up her grave and see her one more time. The urge was so strong that I went out that very night; it was as if I'd completely lost control of myself. But when I opened the coffin, I took one look and got scared and ran home. Later that night, I woke to the sounds of a faint, slow knock at my front door. It was her, don't ask me how or why. But she's back, right back into my life."

Although Jason and I had not had a meaningful conversation in a long time, I still felt that he was my best friend and that I had a responsibility to help him. But my mind was spinning and I was afraid Tasha might be making her slow way to join us outside. Without another word, I turned away from Jason and walked home.

The people of our town are not intolerant, but we are old-fashioned, and we expect people to stay dead once God makes them that way. Jason tried to take Tasha out, to restaurants and to the theater, but enough dirty looks and Jason decided they would be perfectly happy alone in his home.

But they weren't. Jason opened up the hardware store again; say what he might about paying bills, I knew it was to get some time away from Tasha. I own the store right next to his, and while we'd eat our lunches, he'd tell me that death hadn't changed her that much. She still snapped at him. She still loved to argue. She still talked endlessly about her ex-boyfriends. Except now everything took about four times as long.

"There are lots of wonderful, living women in this world," I said to him one day. "Why don't you let me set you up on a date?"

"I can't," Jason said. "Tasha's the love of my life."

"She's a corpse," I said.

Jason nodded. "But when she was gone, I missed her so much it almost killed me. I don't want anything new. I just want Tasha."

"But you're not happy, Jason."

He shrugged. "But I'm not miserable. And I was miserable, so miserable, when Tasha was gone. Even if I'm not completely happy with her"—he paused to shrug once more—"at least it's better than being alone."

Jason got up to leave. I wanted to tell him that he could be happy, that if he'd just have the courage to move on and try something new, he might find true happiness. But Jason was already walking away and I didn't say anything then, and I never got a chance to say another word to him ever again.

Some people say we are a prejudiced town, and Jason took Tasha away to someplace where they wouldn't be judged. But I know it didn't happen that way. Jason would have said goodbye, for one thing, but I've got another reason.

At the cemetery, in the plot where Tasha was buried, the ground has been filled in again. The groundskeeper doesn't know anything about it. Maybe he's lying and Jason bribed him to do it, maybe Jason paid someone else. Does it matter? This is the world of the living; Tasha couldn't stay here forever and Jason wanted to be with Tasha.

Sometimes I think of my best friend Jason and I feel sorry for what happened to him. But it's possible that he's happy where he is. And at least he's not alone.

Part II

Stories of Faith

The Man Who Mistook Himself for a Superhero

FOREWORD

Driven mad by reading too many books of adventure and chivalry, one of my favorite characters in all of literature becomes convinced he's a knight errant, the superhero of his day, and decides to call himself Don Quixote. Whatever else the story started out as—I think Cervantes changed his mind in the decade that intervened between his writing the first half and its superior sequel—by the end of the book, we realize that Don Quixote is a man who wants to make a difference. At his worst, he wants to be important, famous, admired; but at his best, he simply wants to matter and for his life to have meaning—perhaps even to help other people along the way.

While writing the first part of the story, Cervantes may have viewed Don Quixote as nothing more than a silly, crazy old man who's gone soft in the head (and whose antics will soon make him soft with bruises in the rest of his body, too). By the time he wrote the second part, though, I think he fell in love with his character. Don Quixote emerges as a noble spirit, and of all the tragic events that occur to him, none is more tragic than his return to sanity.

As a fellow writer once pointed out to me (to my surprise), this theme—believing you matter and that your life can make a real difference, while everyone else (and sometimes those who care most about you) try to disabuse you of what they see as your embarrass-

ing or dangerous notions of grandeur or importance—emerges of-
ten in my work. The following story, however, is one of my few
conscious attempts to explore the idea. I added a twist to Cer-
vantes's story: here, the main character perceives danger where it
exists in reality and not just in his head; he makes situations better,
not worse; and his power and prowess are real. Given all of that,
I wondered, would his fate be different from Don Quixote's?

THe man in the green-and-yellow costume opened his eyes slowly, first one and then the other. He wasn't dead. He looked down at his chest, then felt around with his fingers as if he didn't believe his eyes. There was no blood, no gunshot wound. And yet he'd been shot; the young ruffian who had pulled the trigger was still standing there, beneath the broken streetlight. He was still holding the gun that had spit out a bullet just moments ago.

Was he crazy?

The look on the kid's face told him he wasn't.

He took a step forward. The kid pulled the trigger again.

There was a small pinch at his chest, as if a needle had been jabbed there—but just that, just a small pinch. He took another step.

The kid pulled the trigger again, then dropped his gun and ran. Walking over to the discarded gun, the man in the green-and-yellow costume picked it up and crushed it in his right hand, as effortlessly as he might crumple a piece of paper.

He looked around; the pretty lady was gone. He felt a pang of anger at that. True, he had told her to flee, but she could have hidden somewhere safe and come out to thank him when the coast was clear.

He put the thought out of his mind. Superheroes didn't save people for thank-yous. Superheroes saved people because it was the right thing to do.

Beneath his mask, he was smiling widely.

So he was a superhero! He'd suspected as much when he'd woken up in the alley behind the Chinese restaurant. He couldn't remember his name, or how he had gotten there, but there was a mirror tossed out in the dumpster and his eyes were working fine.

And what he saw when he looked in the mirror was a golden face staring back at him. There were holes for his eyes, nose, and mouth, and two wing-like extensions to cover his ears.

He wore a green-and-yellow costume made from the same strong-but-flexible material as the mask. His chest was huge, as if he'd been pumping weights since his days in the cradle. Whoever he was, he wasn't someone to be messed with.

As he stared at his impressive reflection in that greasy mirror, he suddenly heard the lady's scream and dashed off toward the sound without a moment's thought for his own safety. He found the young ruffian holding the screaming lady with one hand, and a gun in the other. He felt nervous, but his voice was like thunder.

"Unhand her, ruffian!" he said, and even he was taken aback by the sound of his voice.

Startled, the kid let her go. She fell to the ground but didn't try to get away. If anything, she seemed paralyzed by fear.

"Leave!" he said to her, and the loudness of his voice must have rung a bell in her head. She pushed herself away from the kid, then got to her feet and stumbled off until she disappeared in the darkness.

The kid pointed the gun at him.

"Big mistake, clown," the kid said, and pulled the trigger.

The bullet came at him and he felt a sharp jab at his chest, just above his heart. But he didn't die.

It was later that night that a police cruiser pulled up alongside him as he patrolled the streets. The passenger-side window was open, so the Defender of the Innocent and Helpless—he had not yet come up with a better name for himself, something that rolled off the tongue a bit better, even though he had already given it a lot of thought—said in his booming voice, "No assistance required, Officer."

He kept walking, but the cop car didn't pull away.

"What's your name, friend?" the cop asked. He and his partner were still cruising beside him in the patrol car as he walked briskly, his head swinging side-to-side, scanning for signs of criminal activity.

"I haven't quite decided, Officer," he said, boomingly. Then he stopped suddenly and turned to face them. "Say, what do you think my name should be?"

The cops exchanged looks.

"Okay, fella," the partner said. The car had stopped rolling and he opened his door and stepped out. "Why don't we take a ride downtown?" He started walking toward him, slowly.

The Defender shook his head hesitantly and took some steps backwards. This happened a lot—superheroes were frequently frustrated in their efforts to help people by normal cops. He'd tried to be friendly with them—he'd even asked for their help in choosing a name—but obviously these guys were not about to break with the traditional cop-superhero dynamic.

The first cop was out and walking toward him too. Both had their hands on their side-arms. He didn't want to hurt them and he didn't want to cause a scene. Turning around quickly, he broke into a run. They were following him—he knew that without having to look over his shoulder. But he only heard one pair of pounding footsteps in pursuit; the other cop might have gotten back in the car, to try to cut the Defender off up ahead.

That was the case. The car pulled out of a side-alley and came to a stop, blocking his way. A look over his shoulder showed the other cop following on foot, if a little far back.

The Defender kept running; he knew—somehow he knew—that he could jump over the car. But when he approached the car and jumped—he kept going up. He had pushed on the ground with too much force. He looked back at the ground to see the cops below. He zoomed in on their faces and saw that they were staring up at him with amazement and awe.

He kept floating upward for a few more moments, then, with a twist of his hips, he began to fly forward, his eyes zoomed in on the moonlit city below.

The Defender was on the prowl; criminals and ill-minded ruffians beware.

THe woman who walked through the precinct doors was aston-
ishingly beautiful. She had rosy-red lips, blue eyes, and hair
the color of a detective's shield. She wore a smart business suit
and strode purposefully to his desk.

"Have there been any reports of a man running around in a
green-and-yellow costume?" she said in a sweet but no-nonsense
voice. "He may have been flying around in the air," she added
helpfully.

Under different circumstances, Officer Petrowski would've written her off as a nut-job and had some fun with her. But the report
from the cops on the graveyard shift had already made the rounds.

"Someone fitting that description may have been sighted, yes,"
he said cautiously.

"Under what circumstances? Around which area?" she said,
her voice full of excitement and anxiety. Petrowski wondered if
the costumed guy was her boyfriend. How could he could compete
with a guy who could fly?

"How about you answer my questions first?" he said. "Who
is this guy? Why's he running around in his underwear? What
exactly is the nature of the relationship between the two of you?"
He snuck in the last one, hoping it sounded professional.

"His name is Matthew Peber," she said as if she half-expected
Petrowski to recognize the name.

But the sarge approached his desk before Petrowski could give
the name any serious thought. Petrowski explained who the lady
was and who she was inquiring about, even though he knew the
sarge would take her away. Indeed, the sarge asked the pretty lady
into his office, promising to fill her in on the situation if she'd just
answer a few questions.

Petrowski watched her go with a longing look.

"So he can fly, so what?" he muttered to himself.

LAnding wasn't particularly easy. The slight pain he could deal
with; it was the stumbling that was embarrassing. Superheroes didn't stumble, at least none that he could think of; he didn't
want to be the first.

The Defender was practicing in the dark, empty parking lot of
a grocery store. He'd fly to the roof of the store then run to the

edge and jump off. He could land without stumbling if he paused just above the ground, but he couldn't do it in one smooth motion.

It was daylight by the time he gave up, too tired to go on any longer. Besides, the manager of the store had pulled into the lot and unlocked the front doors, and he probably wouldn't appreciate anyone jumping off his roof during normal business hours.

But where could he go to rest? He thought about other super-heroes, about where they slept when they needed to rest. Spider-Man had Peter Parker's place to crash at, Superman had Clark Kent's and Batman had Bruce Wayne's mansion. Did the Defender have an alter ego? He couldn't remember. It wouldn't do to sleep on the street like some homeless person; that wasn't becoming of a superhero. Maybe he could go to a motel? But he didn't have any money to pay for a room.

Perhaps he could drop by the local police station and ask for a salary. But that wasn't right; superheroes weren't supposed to be on the police-force payroll. Besides, after the exchange with the two officers the night before, he probably wasn't very popular with the cops right now. No, he needed to find a place to borrow money from. He was good for it—a guy like him certainly had marketable talents. Between the flying and the invulnerability to bullets, a ring-leader would pay through the roof to have him work with his troupe. And if he couldn't find a circus in flying distance, he could perform on the street.

The thought of performing made him smile. People's eyes fixed on you as you danced and sung, the very center of their attention—there was something so very appealing about that. If he took up street performing, though, he'd need a hat—a big hat.

As he walked the downtown streets, he realized that though he needed to borrow money, realistically no one would give it to him. He could steal it by breaking into a bank, but superheroes had bad PR as it was; he didn't want to make it worse.

He had the sudden urge to take off and fly, but he pushed the urge aside. He had to walk, to make his presence known, to let honest citizens know that they need not walk in fear anymore and to send a message to dishonest citizens that they better straighten out.

Already he was making a difference. People were looking at him. Some elbowed their friends in the ribs and pointed at him. Whenever that happened, he waved in friendly greeting: he didn't want to be one of those aloof superheroes, but a friendly neighborhood superhero. Honest citizens had to know that they had nothing to worry about when it came to him.

Despite his fatigue, he kept walking, trying to think of a solution to his present predicament. Then it hit him—he didn't have to sleep on the street at all! Had he forgotten that he could fly? He could camp out on the roof of some high-rise.

But a well-timed rumbling from his stomach reminded him that sleep wasn't the only thing he needed. He realized now that he should have spent the night earning money somehow instead of practicing his landings.

He walked into a corner store. A bag of chips and a chocolate bar would tide him over for a while. He was thinking that he could do some favor for the storekeeper in return; mop up the floors or get something off some high shelf. But it was his lucky day: the store was being robbed!

"Hands up, fool," the robber said, turning his gun to point at the Defender. He wore a ski mask, but his voice was obviously that of a young man, probably still in his teens. He was swaying a little and the hand that held the gun was unsteady.

The storekeeper was behind the cash register, on an elevation, standing with his hands straight up, almost touching the ceiling. He had a terrified expression on his face. The Defender shot him a reassuring glance, but it didn't seem to register.

"Hand over the gun, please," the Defender said, his voice like thunder. He held out his right hand with the palm up, realizing too late that he probably shouldn't have said please. "Now," he added roughly.

The Defender stepped forward and the kid stumbled backwards. There was a square wooden platform behind him, supporting a pyramid of cans of tomato soup. The kid tripped over the edge of the platform and fell into the pyramid. Cans bounced off of his ski-masked head; he dropped his gun and brought up his hands to protect his head.

The Defender walked over and picked up the discarded gun. Absentmindedly, he twisted the barrel and bent it back onto itself. The would-be thief started to get up, so the Defender punched him across the face and knocked him out.

"You saved my life," the storekeeper said, coming around and grabbing the Defender's hand and shaking it vigorously. "Thank you!"

"Don't mention it, citizen," the Defender said, his voice so loud that it made the storekeeper flinch. Trying to speak a little more softly, he added, "But perhaps there is a slight reward in it for me?"

A look of cynical understanding swept over the storekeeper's face. He smiled unhappily and said, "Well, I don't have all that much money."

"Actually," the Defender said, "I was thinking more along the lines of a bag of chips and a chocolate bar, maybe?"

The storekeeper stared at the Defender.

"Okay," he said finally, his voice wary. "Help yourself."

The Defender quickly picked out a small bag of all-dressed chips and a peanut-centered chocolate bar. Although he felt embarrassed, he tried to remember that he had earned the food.

"Also a coke?" the Defender said, looking at the fridge at the back.

"Yeah, okay," the storekeeper said, still sounding wary.

A few blocks from the store, the Defender sat down on the sidewalk and opened his bag of chips. He'd had the chocolate bar on the way over.

As he ate, he realized that something was bothering him. He couldn't put his finger on it, but it had to do with what had just happened at the store.

Was it that he had taken the food? But he'd earned that food and besides, he had been hungry. In fact, he'd made a promise to himself that as soon as he had enough money, he'd return to the store and pay back the storekeeper. He was thinking that maybe he should go to the store now and give the man an IOU, when he spotted the police car coming up the street.

There was someone in the back—perhaps the kid who had tried to rob the store.

"Hi there," one of the cops said, as the car pulled up beside him.

"Hello," the Defender said.

"Would you come to the station with us?" the cop asked, trying to make the request sound casual. "We need you to make a statement about what happened back there at the store."

The Defender knew he was lying. They didn't need his statement. He finished his drink slowly, then crumbled up the empty bag of chips.

"Where's the nearest recycling bin?" he asked.

The cop opened the door and stepped out.

"Here," he said, reaching out his hand, "I'll take care of that for you."

"That's very kind," the Defender said, trying to keep his voice neutral. Was it a trick? Would the cop try to grab his arm? He didn't want to take the chance—he wasn't concerned for himself, but for the cop. If the police wanted to hate and ostracize him, that was fine. But he wasn't about to give them any reasons—like a cop with a broken arm—to do so.

He took off before the cop had a chance to make a move. He felt a stab in his leg and almost fell out of the sky. They had shot at him. Non-vitally, but still—they had shot at him. Cops were definitely something to avoid in the future.

But he couldn't stay mad for long. Flying had that effect on him. Effortlessly, he rolled in the air, turning one way and then the other. Turning over once more, he put his hands on the back of his head and allowed himself to glide, watching some strangely shaped snow-white clouds for a while. He closed his eyes, drifted off, and was asleep before another minute had passed.

So he's an actor?" the Mayor asked.

They were in a large boardroom on the fifth floor of city hall. The large wooden table seated twenty comfortably, but extra chairs had been brought in and, Ann estimated, at least forty people were seated around the table. There were at least that many more standing up or leaning against the walls of the room. Sam Miertman sat to her right; to her direct left was the wheezing and coughing Chief of Police. She felt herself leaning away from him, toward Sam. The Chief wore a short-sleeved shirt, and his fat, hairy arm, practically dripping with sweat, brushed up against her every time he shifted in his seat. She repressed a shudder.

"He's not *an* actor," Sam said. "He's Tom Cruise before *Risky Business*, Mel Gibson before *Mad Max*, Brad Pitt before *Thelma and Louise*."

There were blank stares all around.

"He's the next big thing!" Sam said, exasperation in his voice. These people didn't seem to get out to the movies. It was depressing on a professional level if nothing else.

From beside Ann, the Chief of Police said, "And you were shooting this movie when this Peber escaped?"

"He didn't escape," Ann said, making no effort to hide the irritation in her voice. "There was an explosion—an accident— and Matt was flung off set."

The Chief of Police ignored her and pointed a fat, accusing finger at Sam, "This Peber is running around like some lunatic vigilante. This city won't tolerate this kind of behavior, star or no star."

He threw his weight against the back of the chair, which looked like it might give in, and smiled with satisfaction.

The Mayor interrupted Sam's response. Probably for the best, Ann thought.

"What I can't understand," he said, "is how he can run like a cheetah and fly like an eagle, if all this was for a movie?"

Sam looked at Ann. How did one explain the movie business to a politician? How could they explain that they had been given a huge budget to shoot *I, Superhero* but that they ended up using most of the CG effects from Sam's unfinished and unreleased movie, *Hero By Day*?

"We got a lot of money to make this movie," Sam began. "We poured most of it into designing and building the suit. This team of inventors that we hired—DreamMachines, they come with my full and unreserved recommendation—are a bunch of overachieving geniuses. You give them enough money, they can build anything."

He paused, then looked around the table.

"You see," he continued, a little embarrassed, "we needed to get rid of that money, because... because—"

"Because you had to use up the entire budget," the Mayor finished for him, off-handedly, as if he had just provided someone with a word that was on the tip of their tongue. "Or next time around you'd be screwed."

"Yeah," Sam said, sudden relief flooding his face. "Exactly."

The Mayor shrugged. "I've worked in government for a long time," he said, by way of explanation. "So what can we do?"

"The blast from the explosion," Ann began. Eighty eyes turned to look at her. She took a drink from her glass of water and continued, "The blast from the explosion must have caused Matt some sort of temporary insanity. He doesn't mean any harm at all."

Beside her, the Chief of Police made a *hmph* sound.

"I say we take him down," he said, his intertwined hands resting on his belly. "He doesn't want to play nice, fine. But we won't sit around while he flies in our skies and makes a menace of himself. We have a duty to protect the citizens of this city. We won't sit around and tolerate his mob-like extortionist schemes."

"It was a bag of chips and a coke," Ann said fiercely, turning disgusted eyes on the Chief. "Give me a break."

He looked at her with his satisfied smile and said, "Sure, yesterday it was a bag of chips, *a chocolate bar*, and a coke." He emphasized her omission, looking around the table to make sure everyone had caught her slip and his correction of it. "But tomorrow—what will it be tomorrow, or the day after? We can't allow him to run around this city unfettered, above the law, immune to rules and regulations."

The Mayor said, "The Chief is right about that. We must stop him."

There were suggestions from around the table, some more violent than others. The Fire Marshal wanted to use water from high-pressure hoses to force Matt out of the sky and pin him down. The Chief of Police wanted to try some new gluey foam they were developing for the force; it would entangle Matt, and the harder he struggled against it, the more it would constrict him, like a Chinese finger trap. Some guy named Bordan—Ann didn't catch his title—wanted to set up a trap, with a damsel in distress and a net that would drop from the ceiling.

Sam cleared his throat. People kept talking, making suggestion after suggestion, criticizing other people's suggestions and defending their own. Sam cleared his throat a little louder; no one paid him any attention. He cleared his throat once more. Someone beside him stopped talking for a second, then continued.

The Mayor raised his right hand slightly; the room was immediately silent.

"Go ahead, Mr. Miertman," the Mayor said quietly.

"You should know that we have another suit," Sam said. "For the arch-nemesis, Zortran. It's custom built around the actor, though, and he's not here—his first scene isn't scheduled for weeks yet—so we'd have to fly him in from California."

There was a short pause before the volcanic explosion of suggestions, criticisms, and defenses erupted once more. It was as if Sam had never spoken at all.

"What do you think?" Sam said, turning to Ann.

"I'm worried, Sam," she said, her voice low enough that only Sam could hear her. "The longer he's out there, the greater the chance he might do something that'll get him more than a slap on the wrist. And we can't shoot him down or set a trap for him—if he feels his life is threatened, he might do something that'll land him in jail for the rest of his life."

"So you think we should go with Zortran?"

"I think that's best. If Skeet can lure Matt away from the city; if we can get the suit off and bring him back to his trailer and surround him with familiar things; if I could just talk to him for a little—"

Ann stopped speaking, recognizing the look in Sam's eyes. He had reached a decision.

Sam rose slowly from his seat. The clatter of voices continued without a pause and he was completely ignored. Sam looked around the room at the different people. Ann could almost hear him thinking: *I am a director. I directed four thousand extras in the most daring war scene in movie-making history. I got Jerry Pintosh to cry on camera—twice.*

Explosively, he brought his fist down hard against the table. Everyone and everything—the glasses and pitchers of water, the notebooks and pens, the people in their chairs—seemed to jump.

"Thank you," Sam said, using his directorial voice. "Nothing would please me more than to sit here and listen to more of your inane chatter, but if it's all right with you—just this once, for a lark—I'd like to actually do something to resolve this situation before it's too late."

He had been looking around the room at all the faces with their jaws dropped. Now he turned to the Mayor and didn't look away, as if the rest of the room had disappeared.

"Here's what I suggest we do," he said. "We fly in Bronson Skeet from California. He lures Matt Peber away from the city and, when it's sufficiently safe, he overpowers our Don Quixote and forces him out of his suit."

Sam was describing things as if they were scenes in a movie. Ann almost expected him to bring in an artist and have storyboards drawn up. But what if it didn't happen as planned? They couldn't simply re-shoot—this was real life, with real-life consequences. What if something happened to Matt? What if he were hurt?

Sam was still talking. At the end of his speech, he said, pointing a finger at the Mayor, "What we'd need from you is to make sure the city is empty of people at the time this goes down. We'd need you to tell everyone to stay in their homes—to not even stick their heads outside a window. If Matt decides to duke it out in the streets—hopefully he won't, but who knows how far his madness will run?—we don't want any innocent bystanders in the way."

Looking at the media representatives around the room—who had been given silent observer passes into the boardroom—the Mayor said, "I think that can be arranged."

Outside the room, Sam turned to Ann and asked her, "Do you think Skeet will go for it?"

Ann called Skeet on her cellphone. After she had explained the situation and said what she wanted from him, Skeet was silent for a moment.

"Dangerous work, huh?" Skeet said, finally.

"Yes."

"Potentially life-threatening."

"Yes."

"Something could happen to Matt and I'd go to jail for it."

Ann flinched at that but tried to keep her voice level. "Maybe," she said. "Maybe not."

"How much will I get paid?"

Ann said a number.

"I'll be there on the next flight out," Skeet said, hanging up the phone.

O H, thank you!" the mother of the young baby he had just saved said to him, her voice full of joy and relief.

"You're quite welcome, citizen," the Defender said, trying to keep his voice from sounding too harsh. "But please remember that steep hills and baby rollers just don't mix. I may not be around next time."

"Oh, yes, certainly," the mother said, in between kisses of her baby's forehead. "I'll keep a much tighter hold from now on! No more talking on the phone and rolling the baby, I promise!"

The Defender smiled with satisfaction and, with a parting nod to mother and baby, flew away.

As he floated above the river on the city's edge, the Defender finally realized what it was about the thwarted robbery at the store that bothered him so much.

Soon, he realized, there would be no more burglaries, no more murders—no more criminal activity whatsoever. Who would commit a crime knowing the Defender might be watching? Who would act in an uncitizenly fashion when they might face the fury of his mighty arm?

And though that was good news—the end of crime—a part of him couldn't help but feel a little sad at the prospect. Because where would he fit in such a world? If no one needed defending, no one would need the Defender. He'd be useless, forgotten. Like a good therapist, he was slowly putting himself out of work.

But that was foolish, wasn't it? Just now, he had saved a small, cuddly baby from certain death. Earlier that day, he had helped an old woman carry her groceries fourteen blocks and up three flights of stairs. On his way down from that very building, he had stopped two teenagers from fighting and given them a stern lecture about alternate, non-violent means of resolving conflict. His suggestion that next time they had a disagreement, they should discuss it over a game of chess seemed to go over really well.

And besides, there was always the circus.

THat night, he watched two ruffians from the roof of the build-ing in whose mooncast shadow they were hiding. They had stumbled out of the bar across the street and had spent the last ten minutes discussing their plans for mugging someone.

The street was deserted, so the Defender wondered if the two drunks would tire of waiting and go away. But suddenly there was the click-click of high heels on pavement, click-clicks that were getting louder as the lady got closer.

The ruffians whispered to one another, but with his enhanced hearing the Defender heard every word. They were no longer thinking about robbery.

He flew down and landed a bit awkwardly just in front of them. He hoped the darkness sufficiently cloaked his less-than-graceful descent.

"Hello, ruffians," he greeted, his voice booming. "Why are you standing in these shadows? You wouldn't be planning ill-will to honest citizens, would you?"

He hoped they caught the sarcasm in his voice.

"What we's planning to do, it's to kick your ass," the one on the right said.

The Defender listened for a moment—the high heels clicked toward them, toward them, toward them, paused, then clicked away quickly.

He turned his attention back to the ruffians.

"Ruffians," he said, trying to speak sense to them. "You do not want to fight me. You—"

They were on the ground, both of them. One had a bleeding nose that he was clutching like he was afraid it might fall off and the other looked unconscious.

They had moved on him so fast, and he'd just reacted. Obviously he was very well trained in the martial arts, perhaps karate. It was instinct that had taken over when they rushed him. He was sorry they were hurt, but it was their fault and hopefully they would learn a lesson from this experience.

Picking them up and carefully slinging one over each shoulder, he flew them to the nearest hospital and dropped them in front of its doors. Their weight opened the automatic sliding doors and kept them open.

In the air again—flying always put him in a thoughtful mood— he wondered if there were others like him. Were there people in other cities in the world, endowed with special, super-human abilities as he was? Because if there were, he should try contacting them. He might even try setting up a Superhero's Conference. It would be interesting, for example, to hear how other superheroes dealt with the police. There was lots they could teach one another, best practices and lessons learned they could share, anecdotes that only other superheroes could understand and relate to.

But then the thought struck him, running shivers up and down his spine—who's to say that these other superhumans would use their powers for good and not evil? If these super-villains existed— if men and women had the power that he had but not his moral code—it was his duty to seek them out and put a stop to their maniacal plans to take over the world.

He might very well be the only person on earth who had the slightest chance to stop them.

THe thief lifted the old lady's purse with expert swiftness. There were no wasted moves in his actions and not a second of wasted time. The street was incredibly desolate for this time of day—there was hardly anyone in sight, besides the old lady and the man with her purse. The ruffian ran down the empty sidewalk, taking his time as there didn't seem to be anyone around to listen to the old lady's feeble cries for help.

"That purse is really not you," the Defender said. "And it certainly doesn't go with what you're wearing."

The ruffian turned to look behind him but saw no one there. The Defender, flying above him, reached out with a finger and tapped him on the shoulder.

"I'm up here," he said.

Trying to look up at the voice that was harassing him, the ruffian tripped over his own feet and fell headfirst toward the pavement. The Defender reached out to catch him before his head hit the ground, but he was distracted by the sudden appearance of a costumed figure.

Perhaps noticing his distraction, the ruffian tried to make a getaway. Absentmindedly and without taking his eyes off the new figure, the Defender reached out and grabbed the thief by his collar.

"Why don't you pick on someone your own size?" the new figure said, his voice as booming and intimidating as the Defender's. He wore a red jumpsuit, lined with blue stripes and sprinkled with black "z"s.

"Give me just one second," the Defender said, holding up a finger. Turning to the ruffian, he said, "I'll be watching you!"

He flew the purse back to its owner, who—embarrassingly—showed her gratitude with repeated and frequent kisses. He struggled to get away from her grasping arms, assuring her that he was just doing his duty as a superhero. Finally free, he returned to the mysterious costumed figure. On the flight over, he wiped at his mask with both hands to remove any embarrassing lipstick-stains that might have been left there. He landed awkwardly in an out-of-view side-alley.

Walking toward the costumed stranger, he stuck out his hand in friendly greeting and said, "I knew there must be others!"

"I am Zortran!" the man said. "And I am here to destroy you, Alpha!"

The Defender looked over one shoulder and then the other. But he was the only person on the street.

"You have me mixed up with somebody else, Mr. Zortran," the Defender said, finally. "Do you require my assistance in locating this Alpha?"

He wanted to be helpful. He had ambitions of becoming the President of the Association of Superheroes and every vote counted.

After a slight, awkward pause, Zortran said, "You cannot fool me, Alpha! I am here to destroy you and destroy you I will!"

The Defender nodded his head slowly. If Zortran wished to persist in this mad, violent fantasy, maybe a few knocks about the head would teach him not to walk around and threaten other superheroes' lives. Besides, Zortran seemed to speak only in exclamation marks, which was annoying.

Now nose-to-nose with the masked figure, the Defender said, "If you value your life, turn around and never return to this city. If your life is as valueless as it seems, you may strike first."

He took a single step backwards and held his hands at his sides, waiting.

"Not here!" Zortran said. "Follow me!"

Zortran launched into the air, and the Defender launched after him.

It became clear that they were flying away from the city, but why? Was he being led into a trap? Had a band of sinister supervillains joined and plotted the destruction of the mighty and fearsome Defender of the Innocent and Helpless? Was he being led to his own destruction?

It was dumb to go on without more information.

"Hey, Zortran," the Defender called. "Where are we going?"

Zortran flew on without a single look backwards.

Shrugging, the Defender spiraled down and landed. He wasn't going to allow himself to be led into some trap. Zortran kept flying, seemingly unaware that the Defender was no longer following.

He was in a deserted park—everything was deserted, it seemed—when Zortran found him later that day. The Defender had been on a park bench, catching up on some sleep, when he was awakened by that annoying, booming voice.

"I've found you at last, Alpha!" Zortran said.

The Defender got up slowly and rubbed his eyes.

"Hi, Zortran," he said sleepily.

"You are a coward, Alpha! Your belly is well-colored!"

The Defender got up, fully awake. With slow, deliberate steps, he walked up to Zortran and said, his words as slow as his steps had been, "Tell me again. Tell me I'm a coward."

"To call you a coward would be an insult to cowards everywhere! But of all the superheroes I've ever fought, you are the cowardliest of the bunch! You give superheroing a bad na—"

His punch had hit Zortran clean across the jaw and sent him reeling. A follow-up punch dropped Zortran right onto the grassy ground. The Defender stood over him and victoriously placed a foot on the villain's belly.

"You were saying?" he said happily, but suddenly Zortran grabbed his foot and twisted.

Sent crashing to the ground, the Defender tried to roll over and get up. But Zortran was still holding his ankle and his grip was firm, seemingly unbreakable. Zortran grabbed the Defender by the other ankle and began spinning the Defender around his body— once, twice, three times. Then he let him go.

The Defender hit a tree and toppled it over. His shoulder screamed with pain and seemed to have dislocated. But Zortran was already on him, before he even had a chance to move. Lifting him up over his head, the villain flew up a few feet into the air and threw him against the ground.

Although he was winded, the Defender forced himself to his feet—and fell right back down. His ankle was broken.

"Had enough?" Zortran said, coming into view.

With all his might, the Defender swung his elbow at Zortran's right knee and smiled with satisfaction as the villain fell to the ground. He punched Zortran across the face, then jumped on him and held him pinned to the ground, his hands squeezing the villain's red-masked neck.

"Have you?" he said. Dislocated shoulder or not, broken ankle or not—he was good and Zortran was evil. He had a moral obligation to win this fight.

But Zortran had amazing flexibility—he kicked up his left leg and hit the Defender right in the back of the head. Shaken, the Defender loosened his grip on Zortran's neck and that was all the encouragement Zortran needed. Seemingly in one movement, he rolled the Defender over and wrapped his own hands around the Defender's neck.

Zortran was squeezing with all his might.

"I can't—I—can't—breathe," he said, gasping. Was this the end of the Defender of the Innocent and Helpless?

But, amazingly, Zortran loosened his grip.

The Defender kneed him in the groin. He pulled himself up, then hopping on his left foot, he flew away. He needed time to rest and recuperate.

But Zortran wouldn't let him get away. He felt his broken ankle grabbed from behind and screamed out in pain. In the air, Zortran flung him around himself once again—once, twice, three times—and the Defender was sent flying against a brick building.

He tried to twist in the air, but the brick wall came at him too quickly. He hit it head first, then he felt darkness closing in.

"MAtt?"

His eyes slowly came open. His vision was swimming but he recognized the beauty at its center.

"Ann," he said, his throat so dry it hurt to speak. "Hi."

She seemed very happy that he recognized her.

"Do you remember what happened, Matt?" she asked, concern in her voice.

He tried to nod but couldn't—he was in a neck brace.

"Yes," he said. "I think so."

He was in a hospital bed, select body parts wrapped in casts. Flowers and cards filled the small, private room.

"How much do you remember?" she asked.

He was Matt Peber, actor. They had been filming on location for a scene in his latest project when an explosion sent him flying; he landed in a large dumpster behind a Chinese restaurant. When he awoke, he found himself in a costume and believed he was a superhero. A few days later, he had an encounter with Zortran, played by Bronson Skeet. He remembered everything.

"Thank God," Ann said. "We were afraid there might be permanent memory loss or brain damage."

She kissed him on the cheek and he winced in pain.

"I don't know what I would have done if you woke up thinking you were still Alpha," she said. "That was my biggest fear."

"Why?" he asked, trying to prop himself up but failing. "I was helping people."

Ann had a sad look on her face. "No, you weren't," she said. "You were just making a fool of yourself."

"I was helping people," Matt said stubbornly.

Ann shook her head. Did she think he was still crazy? He didn't want her to think that. But he had helped people, hadn't he? That old lady, and the careless mother? And those kids he'd given the talking-to? The storekeeper and the screaming lady held up at gunpoint?

"Are we still shooting the movie?" he asked, trying to change the topic.

Ann shrugged. "Not sure," she said. Was it his imagination or was she suddenly cold? "Maybe later; right now we're on indefinite hiatus."

"Where's the costume?" he asked, trying to make the question sound innocent.

Her eyes narrowed.

"In storage, with the rest of the props, of course," she said, definitely displeased. Then, almost to herself, she added, "I was afraid of this."

Matt reached out his good arm and ran his fingers through her hair.

"Don't be cold," he said. "Please."

Her face softened and she planted another painful kiss on his cheek. "Please tell me you don't think you're a superhero," she said.

"I don't think I'm a superhero," he answered reasonably. "I just think that I might be able to help people, if I were given the chance. That's all."

Ann got up. "We'll talk about it later," she said and left him all alone in the room. It didn't escape his notice that she hadn't kissed him good-bye.

Forget Ann, he told himself. He was surrounded by cards and flowers and candy from other people, people who cared about him. He gathered up the cards he could reach and read through them. Most told him not to feel embarrassed about what happened. It wasn't his fault. It was all in the past, anyway, and worrying about past embarrassments, even when they were played out so publicly, was a waste of energy.

He pushed the cards off his bed.

He picked up the remote control and turned on the television. He surfed through the channels absentmindedly—until he saw his name. There was a panel discussion on him. One of the panelists thought the whole thing had been some kind of advance promotion for the film. All the panelists agreed that, whatever it was, the idea of some guy running around in his underwear, trying to help people, was just hilarious. "I wish I'd been there to see it," one of them said and they all laughed. On another channel, an anchorman related the story with a smirk, shaking his head as if he could hardly believe it himself. The anchorman reminded his viewers that it takes all kinds of people to make up this world of ours.

M Att had a lot of time to think in the days he spent recovering in that lonely hospital room. He had been a fool, hadn't he? He really hadn't helped anyone—except to a good laugh at his expense.

Was he finished as an actor? Could anyone take him seriously again? Or was he forever a laughing stock, the crazy freak who for a short time thought he was a superhero?

It didn't matter. The only thing he could do was to put the whole experience behind him. The public had a short memory and they'd soon forget all about it. Soon, newscasts and editorials would stop ridiculing him. Soon, comedians would take their shots at someone else.

He didn't want to make the movie anymore. It would only serve as a constant reminder of his foolishness, his moment of temporary insanity played out so publicly. He wanted to put the Defender—or Alpha or whatever he was called—as far behind him as possible.

He couldn't wait to tell Ann the good news.

Atheists Against God and the Devil of Destruction

FOREWORD

Some atheists don't have much time for God; the concept of a Creator just doesn't play a part in their thinking and they're able to mostly keep any notions of a supernatural realm out of their minds. Some atheists feel that we as a scientifically-advanced society have outgrown the need for God (or gods).

Some atheists, though, hate God. Not the concept of God, and not religion, not rituals, not hypocrisy or herd mentality (although they may hate some or all of these things as well); they actually hate the God they don't believe in. With one hand they dismiss His existence; with the other, they curse Him. It's a very touching experience when someone who is a self-avowed atheist says to you, in a moment of deep, honest anger, "And anyway—why doesn't He do something *to stop all this suffering in the world?"*

The characters in the next story think they have an answer to that question. They also think they've found a way to stop all the suffering in the world themselves. If that sounds worrisome and ominous to you, you'd be right—as the protagonist of the story is about to find out.

Have you ever seen *Jesus Christ Superstar*? In it, Caiaphas sings of "blood and destruction, because of one man." As I sit and write this under the rain-pelted hotel awning, that line is playing in my mind like a jammed CD. Because I've seen blood and destruction—all of it, not even on account of one man, but because I didn't take that man's name seriously.

Karen, whom I haven't seen or spoken to in more than three years, cautioned me about this. She said I was taking the name of the Lord in vain; there was power in that name, she said, and there was a danger to taking it lightly. I said, "Jesus, Karen, who died and made you the authority—" and stopped as the hurt look on her face registered. I'd done it again; taken the name of the Lord in vain. After a few more arguments, I caved, but half-heartedly. From then on, my sentences to her often began with aborted words and an apology: "Jes—sorry," and "Chri—sorry." Now, sitting here with my jacket pulled over my head so these papers won't get wet, I wish I'd listened to her. And I wish we'd stayed together.

In that happy alternate universe where I never told Karen to pack up her things and leave (it was a figure of speech since we didn't actually live together, but it allowed me to make my dig— "and don't leave your judgmentalism behind, either"—so I took poetic license); in that happy universe, I also never met Susan.

Susan is how the devil would look if he wanted to tempt a man like me. (Why, if I may digress, is the devil so frequently pictured as a hulking monster, horned and red-skinned, bulging with veined muscles, and all but foaming at the mouth with hatred and anger? Why isn't he more often pictured as a sweet-as-sugar blonde with long, tanned legs and boobs the size of bowling balls; a smile to melt icy hearts; eyes blue like a cool, running river; a voice soft as fleecy clouds and smooth as melted caramel? If Satan didn't hide behind illusions, he'd find few customers for his wares). Am I rambling? Well maybe you would ramble too, if a bunch of people were dead and it was all your fault.

Susan, poor thing, got in with the wrong crowd and had her mind scrambled. But I didn't know that the first time I saw her, in a quiet bar in the Market. I saw hair the color of sunflowers, halfway between yellow and brown; I saw eyes the color of a clear sky; I saw a warm, inviting smile.

Soon we were an item; soon she was telling me about her friends who met once a week on Thursdays. The local chapter of Atheists Against God. I thought it was harmless; atheists love to sit around and talk about God, and convince each other in a million different ways that He doesn't exist. But soon I discovered that these weren't really atheists.

"Oh, we believe in God," Mario Tramura told me at my first meeting, with a slight smile as if a child had said something stupid and it was up to Mario to gently enlighten the poor thing. "Where else did the universe come from?"

I raised my napkin and chomped on the head of a deep-fried shrimp to hide my surprise and take a moment to recover. "But you're atheists," I said.

"Yes, but that doesn't mean we don't believe in the existence of God."

"But it does," I said. "That's what the word means."

"Not to us. To us, atheism is the denial of God's goodness. Of all goodness."

Another beer-and-flour-crusted shrimp went into my mouth, a silent sacrifice to my increasing social discomfort. "Is that right?" I said eventually. I looked around for Susan.

Mario didn't notice or didn't care that I wanted out of the conversation. "God isn't good, and no one is good," he said. "Doesn't that make sense of the entire universe, even of the ultimate mystery of its creation? God is a sadist. But a sadist needs playthings. Let there be light and let there be earth and let there be creatures on the earth He can torture. Atheism solves the problem of pain, or the problem of evil or what-have-you, and with it every philosophical conundrum humanity has ever wrestled with."

This isn't so bad, I thought. *He's a Gnostic.* "You should call yourselves Gnostics Against God," I said, relaxing a little. "It's even alliterative." I kept the acronym to myself, and enjoyed an internal chuckle.

"You haven't been listening," Mario said. "Gnostics believe in a supreme God, hidden and good. We're atheists—we deny the existence of good whatsoever."

"Isn't shrimp good?" I picked up my clear plastic cup of red wine. "Isn't this?"

"No," Mario said. "You like the taste? It's an ephemeral good—we deny the existence of permanent, real good. Besides, food and drink extend life, which allows God more opportunity to torment us. And digestion makes your cells work harder, which brings them a step nearer to the end of their natural life. You're a bomb, and with each ticking second you tick a second closer to your own demise. What's good about that?"

"So food is bad because it makes us live longer and food is bad because it brings us closer to death?"

"Something like that."

"So why don't we all dive off a bridge?" I said, hoping to end the conversation as my frantic gaze-search for my beautiful bountiful girlfriend turned up a beautiful bountiful nothing.

Mario slapped me on the arm and said, "Because that would be inefficient." He winked, then walked away, and any relief I may have had was washed away by the words and the wink, which left me standing there like a haunted man.

With impeccably bad timing, Susan found me a few seconds later and asked what was wrong. I hated her. I hated her for belonging to a group of good-hating no-gooders; I hated her for being the reason I had spent ten minutes of my life talking to Mario Tramura; I hated her for being the vehicle through which my brain had been exposed, in mostly unspoken rebellion, to Mario's nihilism. I hated her, most of all, because I wanted to bloody Mario's face and show him how good some things in life could be (like ice on a bruise or aspirin in the body)—I hated her because I knew that if I did that, she'd break up with me and I hated her because I didn't want her to leave me.

"I'm not feeling so good," I said. "Maybe something I ate. Can we go home?"

"Sure we can," Susan said.

We drove home in silence. I wanted to ask about her Atheists Against God friends, but I didn't for fear of losing her. This sounds petty and vain in the cold, harsh light of day, but I liked the way people looked at me when we walked through the mall hand-in-hand, or when I sat across from her in an expensive restaurant when we were both dressed up. Actually, I don't know where I'm getting this notion of the cold light of day because right now it's night, dark, gloomy, and wet. It's raining so hard that maybe there isn't a point to writing this; maybe I should find Noah and lend a hand with the boat.

But here I am anyway, scratching on this pad of half-sheet, hotel letterhead paper with this hotel-stamped blue pen. I'm writing as quick as I can; sooner or later the police will find me and—I've seen enough cop shows to know—they'll want me to write it all down. So I am, and doing it before they can pervert my thoughts with their lies of cold reason. And I'm sorry for my shaky script, but I can't stop trembling.

I was saying that I didn't want to confront Susan about Atheists Against God. But one day a few weeks later, while using Susan's laptop to check my email, I saw a document titled "Catechism (draft).rtf" on her desktop. I was curious to know what a catechism was, so I double-clicked. The document (when it finally loaded—this was Windows) contained a series of questions and answers, like this:

> Q: What do we believe?
>
> A: We believe in God, but not in good.
>
> Q: If God is evil, is the devil good?
>
> A: This is a heresy. There is no good—not God, not the devil, not anyone or anything anywhere.
>
> Q: What is the purpose of life?
>
> A: To poke a stick in God's eye.
>
> Q: How?
>
> A: By taking away his playthings. More than that, by taking away his playbox.

Those words, and the memory of Mario's wink they brought back, scared me into the potentially relationship-ending argument I'd tried to avoid. The funny thing is that Susan wasn't a kook when you talked to her. Her conversations were normal. *Where do you want to have lunch tomorrow? We absolutely must see this new Johnny Depp movie. My hips are too wide. I've never liked broccoli.* It was Karen, with her talk of love and forgiveness and happy heaven and horrid hell—it was always Karen who seemed to me a little kooky.

But that day, after spying on Susan's catechism-in-progress, I told her that her chosen life philosophy made me uncomfortable.

"Deal with it." She sat curled up on the couch, holding her smooth legs at the ankles.

"It's morbid," I said. "And wrong."

She sighed, clicked off the TV, and turned to face me. "It's the only philosophy that explains why the world is the way it is. School shootings. Child-molesting priests. Suicidal terrorists killing innocent people. Earthquakes and tsunamis. If God is good, is He powerless to stop these things from happening? To stop all this suffering before it starts? But how can God be powerless? And if it's the devil who's good, why doesn't he help us? No—the only thing that makes sense is that they're all rotten; and God is the rotten root of everything."

I didn't have an answer for her; or maybe I did, but didn't want to argue.

There were two other questions in Susan's document. After suggesting we take away God's playbox:

Q: When?

A: When the time is right. Soon, I hope.

Q: And in the meantime?

A: Enjoy life, however ephemeral the experiences. Try not to cause anyone any pain, or you'll be adding to God's pleasure.

In the heat of the moment, I'd focused on her murderous nihilism, but later I reflected that there were worse things to have than a girlfriend who wanted to enjoy life and not cause anyone pain.

Months flew by and the issue didn't come up again until last night. I came home from work in a thank-God-it's-Friday-I-can't-wait-to-veg mood, when Susan said she wanted me to drive her to this God-forsaken—sorry, I mean this beautiful city. Seriously, I love Montreal, I grew up here, and if I weren't in a hurry to get my thoughts down I'd write this whole thing in French.

"What's in Montreal?" Girlfriends past had forced me on shopping trips to this beautiful wonderful city—but driving two hours one way to buy a pair of pants still seems like a supremely silly thing to do.

Susan didn't want to go shopping. The Grand Poo-Bah—which I don't say disrespectfully, but because I don't know his name or real title—had called an international conference of the Atheists Against God. She didn't tell me earlier because she wanted to avoid an argument. I could take her or she could bum a ride.

I drove her; I didn't want her riding with Mario Tramura, who would probably wink at her the whole way. I shouldn't write that about Mario. I guess seeing a person's head ripped off from the rest of his body makes one want to be extra nice to all persons.

We drove down the 417 and listened to a Kurt Vonnegut audio book and stopped half-way at a Tim's for dinner.

Our hotel room was small but nice. The queen-sized bed was tightly hugged by a comforter printed in bright round oranges against dark green leaves. A decent-sized TV sat on top of a wooden stand, and behind the doors of the stand was the controller for a Playstation One. Susan wanted to register with the conference organizers, but I was bored and feeling passive-aggressive, and I said I wanted to stay in the room and play games.

Unlike books and music, video games date very quickly and I was bored with the Playstation before the hour was out. On the TV I watched an old but funny show featuring one of Bill Cosby's stand-up sets. A few hours later, the show had ended but Susan hadn't yet come back to the room.

It was late by this time, maybe ten or eleven, and the brochure didn't have any official Atheists Against God functions until tomorrow's breakfast. I put on my jacket before leaving the room, because this T-shirt I'd changed into is the most comfortable one I own, but not fit for public consumption, even in a hotel. I roamed the halls, looking for familiar faces. Then I went to reception and asked about Susan; they hadn't seen her. I'd been getting anxious, but talking to the nice receptionist relaxed me—ever since I was a kid, I've found comfort in receptionists when staying at hotels. Maybe I thought monsters couldn't come while at least one person was awake and standing guard. Now I know better.

Finally, in the hotel bar, I found someone I knew, and I recognized him more from the way he was winking at the pretty sleeveless bartender than from anything else.

"Mario, have you seen Susan?"

He'd seen her; going into the Grand Poo-Bah's room.

I nodded as if this news didn't floor me and I didn't feel utterly betrayed. "I need to give her an urgent telephone message," I said. "What's his room number?"

Instead of knocking, I tried to run the door down. It didn't budge, but my shoulder aches even now as I write this. The noise made Susan come to the door.

"What are you doing here?" She held the door open at a peek-a-boo crack.

"That's what I came to ask you," I said, managing to grind my teeth and talk at the same time.

She stepped into the hallway and closed the door behind her.

"We're preparing something for tomorrow," she said. "Something very important."

"What is it?" I said, looking at the peephole in the door, but seeing only my own distorted reflection.

Susan's shoulders fell in the way she had when she was about to disappoint me. "I can't talk about it," she said. "It might not even work." Her eyes lit up. "But if it does—oh, if it does!"

"Please tell me what it is," I said. Susan was prey to her mothering instinct and I could get what I wanted by reminding her of a child. "Please tell me. Please."

She took a step closer. "We're trying to raise Satan."

"What?" I forced myself to picture Ouija board pajama parties. Harmless fun; happy, happy. "Why?"

"We do it every five years, before the start of the conference. We got really close the last time, but lost him in the end." She paused. "This has to stay secret, okay? We tell people we'll raise him when the time is right, but in truth we've been trying all along. We just don't want to set anyone up for disappointment."

"But why?" I said, losing my grip on scary-fun Halloween parties. "Why are you trying to raise him at all?"

"Because he's the devil of destruction, of course," Susan said. "If we can raise him, we can use him to destroy the universe."

When her nihilism was an abstract and theoretical way to pass a Thursday night with a few friends, I could put up blinders and enjoy the way she smelled like soft citrus. But things had gotten concrete and very real and I realized that my girlfriend, pretty and sweet as she was, was also a maniac.

Even so, I tried to level with her. "He doesn't have that power," I said. "He can't destroy the world."

"According to what?" she said, a patronizing smile on her lips. "The Bible? You forget that I don't believe that stuff."

I turned to walk away, to return to my room and write a letter addressed "Dear Susan." In an instant, I'd decided to drive home this very night, and leave her to Mario or whoever else was willing to put up with her murderous mania. In another moment, I would've been in the elevator and six dead people would still be alive. But before that moment could come, Susan and I heard excited noises from inside the room. We looked at each other, then we both ran in.

The first thing that hit me was a wave of heat from the candles set all around the room. Then I saw five people—three men, two women—dressed in casual clothes, standing in a circle, holding hands, trying to hum something but interrupting themselves with their own excited exclamations ("We're doing it; we're really doing it this time!"; "Shut up and chant!" from a silver-haired older gentleman who must have been the Grand Poo-Bah).

Susan ran to take her place along the circle's perimeter. I stood near the door and tried but failed to see why they were so excited.

Suddenly I glimpsed something. A great gray blob was materializing in the middle of the circle. The shape was indistinct, like the faded print on an old, many-times-washed T-shirt. But the round form was becoming more distinct the more they chanted.

Here's another way of picturing Satan: a tall, gaunt, vampiric skeleton wrapped in rotting gray flesh and a crooked, snarling smile that makes you want to agree with Atheists Against God and give up all faith and hope in goodness. In this image of Satan, he's the embodiment of distorted humanity, more monstrous than monster, and monstrous not from his unknown shape but by its striking familiarity.

Almost as soon as he took solid shape, he began to fade again and the chanters started to lose heart. The silver-haired man tried to shout encouragement in-between his desperate chanting.

I wish I'd walked away or kept my mouth shut. But what happened, as I stood there staring at this fading monstrosity and thinking to myself that these people were desperate to bring him back—what happened is that I said, soft as a whisper, "Jesus Christ."

Suddenly Satan was solid as steel and his eyes flew open. Twin flames burned in there, and it seemed they burned just for me. His arms had been wrapped around his body and drawn-up legs, but now he stood to his full height, which was more than seven feet.

"Keep chanting!" the silver-haired gentleman said.

Satan threw out an arm like a whip and the man's head flew across the room and hit a wall, splashing blood and guts everywhere, including on me. The next five deaths happened almost at once, while I was too fear-frozen to try to help or run away and save my own skin. Satan picked up the two other men by their heads—they were still trying to chant him back into submission—and rammed them into each other with so much force that nothing but mush survived of them from the neck-up.

The girls lost it then and screamed their terror. Satan punched one through the head, making a fist-sized hole where her face used to be. He picked up the other—who had fallen into the fetal position in a corner—and slammed her into the floor, just about flattening her. Then—then he killed Susan. You'll know how if you've been in the room.

I wanted to run away, I wanted to scream, but I stood and stared at the flames looking at me through Satan's sockets. It seemed to me that even as he killed those people, his eyes never once left my own.

With two quick steps he was on me. I fell away, dropped to the ground, closed my eyes, raised my hands (as if these puny things could ward him off), quick-crossed myself in my mind, said, "Lord Jesus, help me," and waited to die.

Eventually I opened my eyes. Satan was gone, but the bloody walls and corpses weren't. The hideousness of everything hit me and I ran—into the hallway, down the stairs, through the emergency exit door, and out into the rain and the shiny downtown Montreal streets.

There. I've avoided getting to this part, but now it's done. I think writing this has actually been good for me. Don't get me wrong—I know that if I hadn't cursed and made Satan crazy, he would've faded away and maybe the Atheists Against God never would have been able to call him, not in a thousand years. Six gruesome deaths is a heavy burden of guilt to bear. And yet, I find I'm not trembling anymore.

You folks are sure to find me soon; I heard sirens many pages back. But it's okay—I'm basically done.

I wonder if you'll believe me. Probably everyone will think I invented all of this to cover up six murders or lay the groundwork for an insanity defense. But what motive do I have to kill anyone, least of all five strangers and Susan? And how could I punch through a person's head, or crumble to dust two skulls? Besides, there's a hotel full of crazy people who'll corroborate most of my story.

If I'm not arrested on six counts of murder—and to be honest, I'd arrest and execute me on the spot if I were someone else, so I wouldn't even have to think of the other possibility—but if I'm not arrested, I'd like to call Karen and see what she's up to. Maybe she'll let me buy her a hot cup of lemon tea, which was her favorite. At the very least, I owe her a few heartfelt apologies.

Blink

FOREWORD

Donnie Darko *is a 2001 movie about a young man who is called out of his house in the middle of the night by a giant rabbit-man, which ensures that the young man is not in bed when an airplane engine crashes through the roof and falls into his bedroom. The horrific rabbit-man causes Donnie to commit a series of crimes, from flooding his school to setting fire to a neighbor's house. But because the school is closed, Donnie meets a girl and falls in love; and when the firefighters go into the neighbor's home, they uncover a horrible secret. It's a strange but interesting movie, best seen with a couple of friends so you can spend the rest of the night puzzling out what exactly it means (and although it's not really the kind of movie one can spoil, skip the next paragraph if you haven't seen the movie and don't want to find out what happens).*

When Donnie goes back in time at the end of the movie and is in bed when the airplane engine falls on him, I thought I knew what the movie was about. Donnie was never drawn out of bed by the rabbit-man, I realized; when he saw the ceiling of his bedroom rip open and knew he would die, he (or his subconscious) allowed him to play out a fantasy where he could fall in love and be a hero. Of course that isn't at all what the movie is about, as another moment of reflection proved obvious. Still, the idea of a person who knows he will die but wants to die happy, and whose subconscious concocts a bit of fantasy to make sure that happens, was powerful and wouldn't let me go. So, finally, I sat down to write it myself.

As so often happens with writers, that's the story I set out to write but, as you'll see, it isn't quite the story I ended up with.

M Ost nights when he couldn't sleep, Jeffrey Williams walked around his building complex for as many times as it took to work off the nervous energy keeping him out of his bed. On this night he ventured out, entering neighborhoods he'd be uneasy to walk even in daylight—but he felt depressed, which made him feel careless, which made him keep walking.

He heard the lady's scream as just a noise; it sounded like the screech of tires. He froze, listened again, and with the second scream he recognized the yell for help. A third scream and he recognized more words. "Someone," and "please."

He turned around and started walking quickly back to his apartment. Why hadn't he brought his cell phone? His heart drummed; it was such a bad idea to go out so far, he knew what these streets were like—

He tripped over something and fell over. Face-down in a dirty puddle of rainwater he thought about what he was doing. Being a coward. Being selfish. Living his quiet, safe life. All the anger and self-loathing came rushing back.

He pushed himself off the ground, feeling suddenly energized. He walked back down the street, following the sounds of the struggle. A loud crash startled him; it sounded like the slamming lid of a dumpster.

Jeffrey ran down the street, turned into the alley. It was dark; the moon was full and bright, but the alley was in the deep shadows cast by the two buildings.

His eyes took a moment to adjust, then he saw the large shadowy figure on the ground by the dumpster, undulating.

"Stop!" he yelled. He ran over and kicked the top of the figure as hard as he could. The figure split in two lengthwise; Jeff kicked again.

The man screamed in pain as he rolled off the woman. Jeff knelt beside her. Her clothes were torn, her face was soaked in blood, twin cuts ran down her cheeks like tears. But she was alive, breathing.

Jeff looked up at the man; he was still on the ground, moaning in pain.

"I'm here to help, OK?" Jeff said. "Come on, arm around my shoulder. That's it."

He pulled her to her feet. She was saying something, but her voice was so soft now that Jeff couldn't make out any of the words. He wasn't sure she knew what was going on.

"We're getting out of here, miss," he said. "You're going to be okay."

The sound of a man cursing made him turn around, and he almost dropped the half-limp lady. Her attacker had gotten to his feet; he looked unsteady, but most of all he looked angry.

Jeff grabbed the woman by the shoulders and yelled into her face to get out of there, then just about launched her down the alleyway. He saw her almost topple over, then gain her feet, look over her shoulder—"Go!" he yelled.

Suddenly he felt as if one of the building's brick walls had detached itself and struck him. He spun, fell to the ground, found himself staring up into wild eyes.

"Ready to die?" The alcohol was so heavy on the man's breath that Jeff tried to turn away, but his jaw was being held in a grip like a vice. "You ready to die, big hero man?"

He saw a flash of silver; a blade; a knife-blade reflecting a random light, raised above his attacker's shoulder, ready to swing down and slice his throat. He opened his eyes wide, saw the satisfied, eerie grin on his attacker's face, then closed them as tight as he could and waited for the strike... waited for the swoosh down, waited for something cold and wet to touch his skin, waited for something sharp to cut into the side of his neck, waited to bleed out in a dark alley, coughing up blood from his carved-out throat, friendless and alone, his one attempt at a decent act ending in senseless tragedy.

Jeff opened his eyes, surprised that he was alive, surprised that it was morning, and surprised that a child was staring down at him.

"You drunk?" the kid said in a conversational way.

"I'm alive," Jeff said.

"Yup." The kid stepped back into the shadow cast by the big blue dumpster.

"What are you doing?" Jeff said, sitting up.

"Hiding. *Shoosh*, OK?"

Jeff crawled into the shadow. "Who from?"

"Kids from school. I wait here till they go by. They pick on me if I try to walk with them. Or in front of them, or behind them if I don't wait long enough. They don't like me."

"Why not?"

The kid shrugged—the slightest shrug, as the bulging backpack he wore weighed down his shoulders.

"What if I walked you to school, would that be okay?"

"No. I'm not supposed to talk to strangers." The kid peeked around the dumpster. "I think that's enough time."

Jeff watched him walk away, a scrawny, hunched-over Atlas, and wondered what he was supposed to do now. Go home? Go to work? What did you do, when you were supposed to cough blood from your slit throat and die, and instead you wake up in an alley feeling more alive than ever?

Jeff's young friend hadn't waited long enough after all. He came flying back into the alley, landing on his backpack and looking like a startled turtle trying to regain its feet. Jeff heard the cackle of bullies' laughter, and he broke into a run.

"You okay?" he said, helping the kid to his feet, then turning his attention to the other kids—three of them, and big kids indeed. One was a giant blob of a kid, almost all stomach with a head plopped on; another was tall and skinny; and the third looked like he spent more time in the gym than in school. All of them looked at least twice his friend's age.

"Hey, Stan*ley*, what's this, you got yourself a boyfriend now?" Muscles said, before turning to Jeff and saying, "He's too young for you, perv. You're a watchomacallit. Watchomacallit, Pike?"

The tall kid said, "A pedo. He's a pedo."

"Yeah," Muscles said. "Stop being a pedo! Stanley's too young for you." He looked over his shoulder to add to his friends,

"Looka'this, freak's walking around in pajamas."

"You guys should leave now," Jeff said, trying to ignore their laughter, but unable to control his voice from cracking a little. Why did he feel so intimidated? These were just kids, right? But like Stanley said, *big* kids. He forged on, still trying to ignore their cackles, "Don't ever pick on Stanley again."

"You're not gonna piss yourself, are you?" Muscles took a step toward Jeff. "You look like you're gonna piss yourself."

Suddenly Muscles grabbed him by his shirt and pulled Jeff in close, the smile on his face falling away. "Don't you piss on my shoes; keep it in till I finish telling you this. I think you're a crazy person who doesn't know enough to change into normal clothes before going outside. So I'm gonna let you go without hurting you, and you can turn around and run away and tell your momma all about this and get her to clean your undies. *OK?*"

Such angry eyes for such a young person, Jeff thought and realized that he wasn't afraid after all. "You need to let me go now," he said, and his voice sounded like it had never sounded before.

A slow, lopsided smile spread on half of Muscle's jaw-clenched face. "Yeah, you go," he said, dropping his hands. "Go home to your momma."

Jeff straightened out his shirt and said, "And now turn around and walk away, and make sure I don't ever catch you talking to Stanley again."

He saw what happened next almost in slow motion: Muscles's muscular arm struck out, launching a fist to his stomach, but so slowly that Jeff just stared at it. Then the fist made contact. It felt like a tap, like a friend slow-sparring for fun, but Muscles looked as if his hand had been crushed by a cinder block.

"Your wrist is broken," Jeff said, but he wasn't sure how he knew it. He took a step forward—he thought for a moment that he could actually see through the man's flesh, look right at the fracture in the bone. Muscles stumbled back; the look of terror on his face made Jeff feel like a monster.

He watched the group run away. Three bullies, running away from him. He wanted to run after them, chase them down like they'd chased down so many people so much smaller than themselves. Chase them down and teach them a lesson. He felt the power pulsating throughout his body.

Suddenly he realized how hard he was breathing; realized how badly he wanted to run after those guys and tear them limb from limb; realized that if someone saw his face, it wouldn't look like a monster's but like a devil's.

His friend hiked his bag further up his back. "Okay," Stanley said, "thanks. See you later."

Jeff turned back to the alley. What happened in there? What happened to the guy about to slash him with a knife? What happened to those last few nighttime hours? And, most of all, what happened to *him*?

He started walking toward his apartment, to change clothes if nothing else. Was he late for work? He didn't know what time it was; he didn't even know what day it was. Not Saturday or Sunday, anyway; the bank up ahead was open and this branch never opened on weekends.

He started to cross the street and was almost run over. Through the windshield, he saw the driver curse at him and veer away. The dark blue BMW snaked down the wide road, picking up speed, sliding between the two lanes.

"Lucky break, buddy," somebody said, as he walked past Jeff.

"Yeah," Jeff said. Up the street, a car in the westbound lane honked at the Beamer, which was drifting across the yellow line. The Beamer pulled away, but overcompensated and went all the way across the road and up onto the sidewalk. In one instant, Jeff heard the terrified bark of a leashed, trapped dog as if he were standing right beside it, and in the next instant he was standing right beside it, or right in front of it.

The Beamer slammed into him and crumpled, hood to windshield, metal deforming itself into a V to get out of his way.

Jeff wasn't surprised, which shocked him. It seemed the most natural thing in the world for him to stand his ground against a hurtling metal machine, and have the machine come out the worse for the experience. He felt no pain—just very cold, as if his entire body had turned to ice as soon as the car touched him, and in fact, the frost was only now melting from the windshield.

It seemed so natural, as if deep down he always knew this is exactly what would happen if it came down to it, vehicles of the world beware. It seemed so natural—and that something so unnatural would seem natural shocked him to his core; shocked him so much that for the moment he didn't even think about how he'd just run a block in under a second.

The driver of the Beamer had enough sense at least to have worn his seat belt, and he was currently eating a face-full of airbag. Behind Jeff, the dog scratched the side of its head up his leg and emitted a low, long whine.

"You're welcome, Pooch," he said. "Now step away from my leg."

A small crowd was gathering. The dog's owner came running out of the corner store and untied him from the no-parking-monday-to-friday sign.

"Thanks for your help," she said off-handedly to Jeff, then: "Come on, Muffin, off we go."

"Someone call the cops?" Jeff said.

A young girl in a pink jacket held up a cell phone.

When they arrived, the two cops surveyed the situation, then one of them said, "OK, we'll take it from here."

"OK, see you guys," Jeff said.

Feels perfectly natural, Jeff thought, *as if this isn't the first time I've run like a bolt of lightning and stopped a car with nothing more than my good looks.* And yet there was still enough self-consciousness in him to realize that it shouldn't feel so natural, that in the real world people didn't do that sort of thing and live to tell about it.

On a whim, he crouched and—looking up—launched himself into the air. At first he thought it hadn't worked, then he looked around and realized that he stood on the roof of the bank, standing beside the large metal M. He peeked over the ledge, took a look at the figures below, and stepped quickly away. Maybe he could fly, but heights still made him nauseous.

It was several days later that he figured out what was going on. In those first few days, the *unnatural* feeling was so faint that he often forgot about it; and the *natural* feeling was so strong that he didn't question it.

But one night, flying above the city, he saw mountains of white smoke rising from the assisted-living home. He looked through the smoke and fire, through the walls and doors, and saw that four people were trapped in the cafeteria. Two fire trucks and a dozen firefighters were trying to get the fire under control, but Jeff knew they wouldn't—not in time to help the people trapped inside.

He landed and dashed into the building, brought out two of the residents, then dashed in again and brought out the other two.

Firefighters were already taking care of their patients, offering them bottles of water and leading them to some patrol cars so they could sit down, but one resident—an old lady who reminded Jeff of his grandmother—put her hand on his arm.

"Thank you, dear," she said, and Jeff could see she wanted to kiss him on the cheek; he leaned over to make it easy for her. She kissed him, smiled, wiped away the makeup her lips had left on his cheek and said, "You're an absolute dream."

Jeff watched in stunned silence as she was escorted away. *An absolute dream, of course.* He understood, and it was the same sense of relief he felt toward the end of a good mystery novel, when enough clues were laid out in front of him that he saw the answer. But the old lady's words were the answer to not one but many riddles. Where was he? Why could he fly? Why could he take twelve bullets in the chest and not feel any pain?

An absolute dream.

"You okay, Superman?" one of the bystanders said.

Jeff turned around and smiled reflexively before he realized who had spoken to him. It was his scrawny Atlas, the little kid he'd helped with the bullies.

"Stanley, right?"

The kid nodded, a soft smile on his face and his deep, intelligent eyes searching Jeff's. Something was very different about him; something hard to pinpoint, but as if Stanley had stepped off the stage; as if the Stanley he'd met before was acting the part of a child, and this was the real Stanley, a Stanley with a knowing smile and probing eyes.

"You realize this is all in my head, Stanley?"

The soft smile turned into a laugh. "Is it?"

"I just realized it. But it's the key that fits, it answers everything." Behind him, firefighters wrestled with the flames, their shouts to each other barely audible over the roar and crackle of the fire as it feasted on the building. "The only thing is—it doesn't feel like a dream, it feels real. I don't mean real in the sense that a lot of dreams feel real, even when you're dreaming, but real in the sense that consciousness is real."

"What's the last thing you remember before the dream?"

"I. . . I don't remember anything before the dream," Jeff said, holding up his hands. "I woke up in an alley and saw you. I"—he stopped, the remaining words dying in his throat, as images flashed in his head. Two dark figures wrestling, a woman fleeing a dark alley, the flash of a silvery object. The final mental picture was of him, not immortal but dying, not flying above the city but sprawled out on the wet asphalt of some alley, and the asphalt was wet with his blood. "I'm dead," he said. But that wasn't right—his throat hadn't been cut; that final mental picture was a projection of the future.

"As soon as I regain consciousness, I'm dead," he said, with certainty.

Stanley looked at him with a curious stare, but Jeff knew he was right—knew that everything he had experienced since waking up in the alley, everything he now experienced—that all of it was happening in the brief moment it took for him to close his eyes before the knife touched his neck. As soon as that moment was over, he'd open his eyes and find himself in the dark alley. But what was the point? What was the point of this dream?

It was only when Stanley answered that Jeff realized he'd vocalized the question. "Is it a dream?" he said. "What else could it be?"

Jeff looked over his shoulders; the building had collapsed on itself, but the firefighters were getting the fire under control. No one paid him or Stanley any attention.

"It could be random firings of a brain that knows it doesn't have long to live," Jeff said, because that seemed most obvious. But his own sense of logic and the look on Stanley's face made him quickly add, "No good, I know. This is all too consistent and purposeful—too non-random—to be random." He suddenly felt very tired, and sat down on the ground cross-legged. Stanley sat beside him, and played with the laces on his runners. He seemed to be waiting for Jeff to figure out what Jeff was convinced Stanley already knew.

Eventually, a smile spread across Jeff's face and he started to laugh. "Of course. It's a gift."

Stanley raised an inquiring eyebrow, a comically mature, almost professorial gesture from such a young face.

"It's a last happy dream," Jeff said. "A gift from the universe"—he saw that look again on the professor-kid's face—"no, wait; I know the universe is a thing and can't bestow gifts anymore than it could send an email. A gift from...me, to me. I knew I was about to die, so in that instant...I gave myself a vacation in my head, a new life—the happy wish-fulfillment life of a superhero."

"And why would you do that?" Stanley said, smiling.

"To die in peace? To die content, right? One last chance to live a life better than the life I lived." But even as he said the words, he felt they were untrue. Could he really trick himself—could his brain, without his knowledge, concoct a strategy for giving him one last happy dream, and trick itself into believing the lie? And even if it could, what was the point? What did it matter if he woke up happy or sad—if he woke up simply to die?

If not the universe, if not himself—

"I don't believe in God," Jeff said, his eyes suddenly growing wide as a dawning realization made him turn cold.

"But if you did?"

Jeff looked at the little kid, thirty years and two feet his junior, and yet he wanted to answer correctly—or at least intelligently. "God is giving me this dream? God wants me to be happy?"

"You don't seem very sure."

"I'm not; it doesn't make sense." Jeff felt his shoulders slump; he picked up a small pebble and twirled it in his hand. "If there's a God, presumably there's an afterlife. If there's a good afterlife and I'm going to it, who cares that I have a dream of happiness, if I'm headed to eternal happiness? And if there's a bad afterlife and that's where I'm going... well then this would all be pretty mean-spirited of Him, I think. If God exists, He wouldn't be playing games, would He?"

"I don't know," Stanley said. "What else could it be?"

Even though he didn't believe in God, Jeff voiced the thought that had sent chills through his body. "Maybe it's a test."

The kid smiled. "A test? You mean, maybe God wants to see what kind of person you are? So He gives you all the power in the world—but you don't rob banks, you catch bank robbers. You don't bully anyone, even though you could bully anyone you wanted; you defend the victims of bullies. You don't start fires, you save people from them."

"Well if life is a test, and this dream is part of that test, I hope He judges me on the dream. I spent my childhood as a punching bag... bullies picked me out of a crowd like I was wearing a sign. It turned me into a... a coward. I avoided all confrontations, anything that could be at all dangerous... lived my life like a walking plant."

"But stripped of all the circumstances that made you exhibit those behaviors, and given ultimate power, you used it for good. You talked about wish-fulfillment, but becoming all-powerful and taking revenge on everyone who dared to hurt or insult you... that could be the object of wish-fulfillment too. You could've become a supervillain, but you chose to become a superhero."

Jeff stared at the asphalt. After a while, suddenly aware that the night had grown cold, and that he should get this child back to his parents, he said, "Come on, my wise little friend. I've enjoyed talking to you tonight."

"I'm glad—the next little bit won't be easy for you." Stanley stared at something just behind Jeff, and in his eyes Jeff saw the reflection of a silvery object.

He turned his head and the knife cut across his throat, a precise, practiced stroke. There was no pain, at least; or so much pain that Jeff lost his ability to feel any of it.

His attacker leaned into Jeff's face; the smell of booze, stale and rancid, filled the air between them. "Was it worth it, huh? Was it worth playing the big hero man?"

Jeff tried to answer him, but the words were drowned out in the blood pouring out of his throat and he only made wet, gurgling sounds.

"Was it worth it, huh?" Was that the drunk still talking, or an echo of his voice playing in Jeff's mind? He couldn't tell. The smell of booze was gone, and his vision was even darker than before.

"Was it worth it, huh?"

"It... was," Jeff said, or thought he said, "an... absolute dream."

In the last moments before death, he heard a voice, an old lady's voice telling him that he was a dear; and he felt something on his cheek, something moist. Probably his own blood, but it felt like a kiss, a kiss good-night or good-morning.

The Talent

FOREWORD

I wouldn't be the first person to remark on the parasitic nature of evil. As C.S. Lewis put it in Mere Christianity, *"All the things which enable a bad man to be effectively bad are in themselves good things."*

Setting aside the horrors of the evil act itself, then, the underlying tragedy of evil is that it is goodness misapplied. Evil is not only bad, it's doubly bad; because over and above the badness of the evil act itself, there's the additional badness of the missed opportunity to do good. And if one believes in a good God who created and sustains the universe, then what's missed is not only an opportunity, but a call—a call to do good with the gifts one's been given.

I Used to be a hired gun—with two exceptions. One is I was picky, two is that I never used a gun. The first I can explain easy: the guy had to deserve the dying. The second is going to take some telling and requires what the high-brows call a digression.

The first time I used my talent, it was on my dad. I was eight-years-old, and I didn't know I had it then or even that I had used it, but one moment I heard my bedroom door creak open and the next I heard a loud thump! as Dad fell flat on his nose. I didn't feel angry or sad; I just felt guilty, the way kids do sometimes.

It was just me and Dad in the house; Mom had died in the hospital giving birth to me. Dad used to say she died so she wouldn't have to raise such a bad kid.

I didn't call 911 that night—I just bolted out of the house, with my old school bag already packed with clothes and some chips and cola 'cause I'd been planning on running away. For two years I had planed to run away, but I always chickened out, and ended up eating the chips and drinking the cola and asking Dad to buy more. But I ran that night 'cause I was scared, more scared than I'd ever been before. I bolted out of the house, still wearing my pajamas and clutching that old school bag that had the picture of Spider-man on the front as if it had the power to hide me from the cops. I felt like they were after me—the cops—that they had discovered I'd killed my dad and were coming after me. That night, hiding underneath a rotting wooden bench in a park a few blocks from the house Dad and I used to live in, I dreamt that they'd finally caught up with me. They threw me in a big room and shined a bright light in my eyes and asked why I'd killed Dad. Over and over, "Why'd you kill your pa, boy?" Then, "Fess up, son, we'll go easier on ya if you cooperate." I don't remember dreams most of the time, but I still remember that cop's voice. Rough and grumbling, the voice of a guy who'd smoked cigars since he was inhaling.

I couldn't speak in my dream, couldn't say a single word to defend myself. "All I did was pray," I'd practice during the day, as I hid in dumpsters behind different restaurants and ate what they threw in. "I just prayed, hoped, wished that Dad wouldn't come near me anymore. I didn't mean for him to die." I practiced in case the cops ever did catch me, but also so I could say it in my dream. I had the dream almost every night after I killed Dad for about a month, but I never could say anything to defend myself.

I stopped having the dream the next time I used my talent. It was mid-October and getting cold, and I was behind a small convenience store asleep in a warm spot between pillows of garbage bags. I woke to loud, angry voices. Curious, I followed the sounds. There was an elementary school like I used to go to nearby, four guys standing in its parking lot. I was hiding behind a tree, and I could see them pretty clear thanks to these two tall light posts that hung over them like evil spirits. Two of the guys distracted this other guy while the fourth circled around him and pulled out a knife as long as my arm. I saw it flash out of the guy's pocket, and—insanely—I screamed "Look out!" before I could stop myself.

I didn't even wait to find out if they heard me, I had that much smarts at least. I turned tail and bolted. I fell on a rock before I got too far, and cut myself pretty bad, but I lay there like a corpse anyway, perfectly still, perfectly quiet. But the guys had flashlights and were searching around and shouting back and forth to each other, and I suddenly became very scared and started to panic—and got up and started running again.

They caught me and dragged me back to the school's parking lot, where this guy was on the pavement, bright red blood leaking away from him like water from a hose that wasn't turned off all the way. His tongue was on the pavement a couple of inches from his head. Something solid and bitter worked into my throat; I forced myself to swallow and tried not to think about throwing up.

"That's what happens to squealers," one of the guys said, maybe 'cause he saw that I was staring at the tongue. "Now we're gonna show you what happens to peeping toms."

I closed my eyes tight as I could and tried to take my mind away, like I used to do with Dad. But one of the guys jabbed his thumbs in my eyes, really hard. I heard the other two laughing. Dad used to say that a man that cries ain't a man, but I couldn't help myself. It's stupid, but I was really ashamed that these guys—one poking my eyes with his thumbs, the others standing around and laughing—would think less of me because I was crying.

Although the guy had forced my eyes open, my vision was blurred—whether from the tears or the pain, I don't know. But I felt something sharp and cold pressed against my throat and realized—almost too late—that it was the knife they'd used to kill the other guy, and now it was my turn.

I dropped them dead, to give you the short of it, like I had done my dad. I curled up in a dark corner in my mind and said, "God, please God, take these guys away." And He did.

Fter that, I knew I'd never need to carry a gun for the rest of my life. When I discovered my talent—when I realized what I was capable of—I went from an eight-year-old scared of just about everything to fearing nothing and no one.

I was a pretty smart kid even at eight, when most kids don't know anything except video games and sports. So I thought I had it figured out—God was paying me back. All the nights I'd trembled in my bed, terrified of my own father, God was now apologizing for and making sure that I wasn't ever afraid again.

I didn't hang around that parking lot too long. I just looked the guys over, the guys I had killed, and felt like the most powerful person in the world. I was so excited I started trembling; I even kicked one of the dead guys in the stomach before I ran away, which I felt sorry about afterward.

I survived pretty well as a kid, eating scraps and sleeping whenever I got tired. I did odd jobs sometimes and made a little money, which I kept in my socks. I'd especially look for moving trucks. Wherever there's a moving truck, there's someone who needs an extra hand lifting boxes and is willing to pay you for it, especially if you're a kid they think won't make too much noise if they try to bilk you. At night, I'd walk through the neighborhoods and pick out what I wanted from their garbage.

Someone that worked for the city found me walking the streets a couple of months later. I ended up in a long string of abusive homes, landing with people that made Dad look like a saint. When they thought I wasn't listening, the Agency people called me the cursed child, because so many of my foster parents ended up dying in their sleep.

I finally landed with a decent old lady who was richer than anyone I'd ever known before. She lived in a great big house that had a pool in the back as big as the house Dad and I used to live in. Kids from the neighborhood would come over to Miss Dimple's house—Miss Dimple is the lady I'm talking about—on Saturday mornings and Sundays after church to swim in her pool.

I spent two years with her, from fifteen to seventeen, and I could tell you lots that she did for me. The short of it is that she made me go to high school and tutored me every night so I could catch up. She died of cancer before she could see me graduate from high school, which made me sad enough that I didn't bother going to the ceremony.

Given my background, it's strange how badly I dealt with Miss Dimple's death. But I didn't use my talent for more than three years after she died; maybe I didn't want to make anyone else feel the way I felt. Young as I was, I knew that even the worst of us have got someone that cares. Someone who'd cry when we died, even after the funeral, and think about us from time to time.

I flunked my driver's license test twice in the next two years. If I kept flunking it, maybe I never would have used my talent again. But the third time was a charm for me. Things were okay at first, when I was just getting the hang of driving, 'cause I was nervous and careful, but after a few weeks with my foot on the pedal, I became easy to irritate.

If someone drove too slow in front of me, it pissed me off. If I saw someone in my rearview getting too close, it pissed me off. If someone cut me off, or even if someone in the next lane drove faster than I was driving, it pissed me off.

One day, I just erupted like a volcano and wish-killed the guy driving the van in front of me and crashed right into him. Killed the kid that was sleeping in the back.

No one blamed me. The cop who told me about the accident said the guy in the van had suffered a heart-attack and that the little kid sleeping in the back had died immediately and had probably felt no pain.

I got out of that hospital as soon as I got the chance, didn't bother with my car or my money or anything, and got as involved with drugs and hookers as a guy possibly can be. Night after night, I stood outside an all-hours theater and robbed people as they came out until I had enough money to get my fix, drugs or girls or whatever I needed that night. But robbing innocent people made me want to jump off the roof of a building every time I did it; I knew I couldn't keep going like that. So I went from using drugs and girls to selling them.

A couple of months later, one of my girls came back roughed up, with bruises on her legs and arms. I found the guy who did that to her; when I left, he was begging me to kill him. But I didn't—after the car accident, I'd promised myself that I wouldn't have any more deaths hanging over my head.

After that, word got around that I was a pretty tough guy and I quit the pimping business to go into the intimidating business: I became a hired bully.

It was around that time that I met Gracie. I was throwing up in some dark alley, which was the way my body always reacted after finishing a job. Gracie followed the sound of my retching to ask if I was all right. When I looked up, and saw her face in the moonlight, I couldn't believe that anything so beautiful could exist in such an ugly place. When she repeated her question, I couldn't believe that someone could have such genuine concern for a complete stranger.

Anyway, I quit bullying after a girl who'd paid me to beat on her boss showed up at my apartment door in two garbage bags, one for her head and one for her body. I found the guy and killed him and the goons he had with him, because I wasn't sure I could take them all in a fair fight.

It wasn't safe to stick around after that—not that I was worried about myself, but about Gracie. Everyone knew she was my girl; everyone knew they could hurt me the worst by hurting her. The thought of Gracie getting hurt—Gracie, who'd never hurt anyone; Gracie, who always had something positive to say, no matter how bad things got; Gracie, who was my only source of light in a dark and lonely world—the thought of her getting hurt was enough to make me want to scream until my heart exploded, and more than enough to get me out of that city.

Gracie and I had some money saved up and we got a small apartment in a quiet neighborhood where no one's in the streets after eleven. I got a job managing a small coffee and donut store, where I had to make sure that there were enough donuts on the shelves and coffee in the pots, and that the bathrooms stayed clean. Gracie got a job as a secretary for some big-time lawyer with his own firm; secretary is what she did before she got downsized and fell into hooking. A few years before she found me puking in the alley that night.

I guess we were both trying to go straight in this new place.

Life got to be pretty good...except for this feeling I couldn't shake, that I was hiding from my destiny. The more I watched the news and the more I read the papers—the more I felt like there were people walking the planet who didn't deserve to live. I began to jot down names.

I became a killer, which is not how I saw it at first. I saw myself as a garbage man, taking out society's garbage day in and day out. At first, if ever I did feel bad, it was because of the thought that there was more scum on the earth who deserved to die than I could possibly get to in my life. But you've got to keep trying, I used to tell myself. Reach exceeding grasp, like that one poet said.

When I killed a guy, did I think that he might have a wife and kids that depended on him? Did I worry that I'd killed a guy who might have come up with the cure for cancer if I'd let him live another week, another month, another year?

I tried not to. I did my homework, made sure the best I could that my mark deserved for me to kill him. It's one of the reasons I became a hired gun, with the two exceptions. I got my clients to do research for me. If they could convince me the guy deserved to die, I took the job.

But every time I killed someone, I wrestled with the fact that no one is all bad. The wife-beating drunk was maybe the nicest person to his mistress.

But you've been given a gift, I'd remind myself each time. *And you have to use it.* The way I figured it—someone or something had given me this talent. There was a reason for me to have it. The best I could do was my best—and hope that things not only balanced, but came out positive.

So I quit my donut store job and started doing very selective contract work. Sometimes it paid very well, sometimes not. Sometimes I loved my job. Occasionally I tried to stop. Sometimes I wished those cops with the bright lights would catch up to me and stop the whole thing once and for all. If it weren't for Gracie, maybe I would've wished myself dead eventually.

My conscience aside, Gracie and I lived well. She waited for me to marry her; I just loved waking up every morning to see her face. We went to movies and out to dinner and showed our faces at boring office Christmas parties. We lived like that for three years. Then God decided to kill Gracie.

Miss Dimple used to say that everything happens for a reason. I don't know if that's true always, but it was true in this case.

Gracie and I were taking a walk in a park near our apartment, something we did almost every Friday night in those days. Lately, my work had been causing friction between us. Gracie didn't know about my talent, of course. She thought I was beating on people, like in the old days. And she didn't like it, to give you the short of it.

"We don't need the money," she would say.

"I don't do it for the money," I would say.

"You might get hurt," she would say.

"I won't," I would say.

Just like that, on and on. That Friday night, as we walked, she started in on me again.

"I don't like it, okay?" she said. "I don't like the thought of you going around hurting people for a few bucks."

"I told you," I said. "I don't do it for the money."

"Then why do you do it?"

How many times had I asked myself that question? And what would she think of me if I told her the truth? What would she think of me if I told her, "Because killing is who I am"?

"Because some people deserve to get hurt," I said instead.

"Why do you get to decide who deserves to get hurt?" she asked, but I couldn't answer that.

"It's like this," she said. "There's so much ugliness in this world, so much evil, and so many people causing hurt and pain. Contributing to it is like throwing a glass of water into the ocean. You might make a few ripples, but that's about it, and no one re- members that you threw in the glass after a while. You might as well not have thrown it in at all, because you really haven't made a difference. Whereas, if you do good, even if it's just a little bit, you've made a big difference, because your drop of water is being added to such a small amount. You're making a difference, see?"

Gracie sometimes talked like that, with metaphors and similes and sometimes I couldn't understand her but this time I did.

She asked me to promise that I wouldn't take on another job. I did, but I didn't intend to stop killing people—I was pretty sure I didn't have it in me to stop, whether I wanted to or not—only that I wouldn't do it for money anymore.

The next morning, I was in the shower when I thought I heard her moving around.

"You're welcome to join me," I called out, but she didn't answer.

I turned off the water, wrapped a towel around my waist, and went back to the bedroom.

She was dead. I'd had enough experience to know a lifeless body when I saw one. The first thought that came into my mind was that God was punishing me for taking away all those people's lives.

I didn't call for an ambulance—all they'd be able to do was tell me why and when and how she had died, all of which I didn't want to know just then.

I knelt down on the bed beside her, and begged God to give her back to me. I prayed, "God, please God, Gracie's all I got in this world and life ain't worth the living without her." For a brief, desperate moment, I thought that maybe my talent worked both ways—if I could kill someone just by wishing it, couldn't I bring them back by wishing harder than I'd ever wished for anything before?

I begged and prayed and cried for maybe three hours, but Gracie didn't twitch an eyebrow. I was exhausted after all that, and I fell asleep, right on her chest.

IT's hard to swim in the ocean, I thought. All these waves. I tried to keep my head above water, but another bobbing wave came along and threatened to pull me under. I fought my way back up, broke through the surface of the water, and gasped for air.

But what was I swimming toward? I looked around, circling in the water, but couldn't see anything. Then a sound—like the beating of soft drums—made me look in a direction and I saw it— land!

I swam with a purpose, toward the green and brown of the coconut trees. The swelling waves tried their best to pull me under, but they only managed to slow me down. My gaze was fixed on the trees standing tall and distinct against the cloudless blue sky. I swam toward that island, encouraged by the steady sound of native drums. Even the trees seemed to be cheering me on, as they waved in the wind.

I woke up only slowly, to the up-down bobbing of Gracie's breathing and the soft sound of her beating heart.

"I didn't want to wake you," she said, looking down at me and playing with my hair. "You looked so peaceful."

I felt peaceful.

And I became peaceful, too. Not that I stopped using my talent—it was a gift, and I had to use it the best way I knew how. I still killed after that, but I didn't kill people anymore.

I killed the cancer of a patient in the hopeless section of the hospital, I killed the pain in the back of an eighty-year old man, I killed the HIV in a kid whose mother almost made me want to break my rule about killing people.

In all, I've only got one complaint, which is saying a lot about a life, and it's that there's more people in the world who deserve to be healed than I can possibly get to in the time I've got on this earth. But while I'm here, I've got to keep trying, reach exceeding grasp; dribbling a little good into the world, one drop at a time.

Part III

Stories of Love

They Came From Ooter's Place

FOREWORD

"They Came From Ooter's Place" is the first story of mine to be paid for and published.

When I was a teenager, I suffered from rather severe facial acne. Facial acne is weird: you don't see it unless you're looking in a mirror, so often you forget that you even have it. But when you're conscious of your acne, you can't imagine that anyone who looks at you could be seeing anything else. On what must have been one of these "acne-conscious" days, I had an idea for a story about a boy suffering from a progressively worsening case of acne. One day while sitting in his high school's cafeteria eating his lunch, he becomes aware that everyone is staring in horror at his face. His pimples are growing, maybe even glowing. Then they pop explosively, and spaceships come flying out of them, shooting lasers at his classmates, killing everyone and especially the girls he wanted to date.

Gross as it is, I still like the idea (and the title I came up with: "They Came From Ooter's Face"). The problem, of course, is what kind of punch could a spaceship tiny enough to fit inside a pimple actually pack? Lasers notwithstanding, couldn't one just swat them down and out of existence? So I thanked my brain for the idea but decided to pass... except the notion of an alien invasion wouldn't go away.

You don't know Ooter, most likely. You don't know about the invasion, neither, but that's why I'm telling you about it. Anyway, Ooter used to be my best friend, and he didn't know about the invasion till after it was too late, so there's no use in trying to blame him for anything I'm about to tell you. Like I said, Ooter was my best friend once, and he wouldn't want to hurt anybody that never hurt him. Ooter's huge—taller than my dad, actually. If he's around, the school librarian will ask him to reach books for her, on account of not wanting to haul out the ladder. Also on account of her being afraid of heights. I been on the ladder once, it's not so bad. Anyway, Ooter's huge, so all the bullies leave us alone, even though he never once beat any of them up.

Like I said, Ooter didn't know about the invasion at first, and I know you're thinking that's on account of him being a little slow, but there's no truth in that, because, you know, he figured it out pretty quickly when he got the chance. Which I forgot to tell you— Ooter was a little slow some times. His family had moved down here from Germany or someplace like that, and Ooter was having a lot of problems with English, even though his parents could speak it fine.

So even if he did know about the invasion, which, like I said, he didn't, he couldn't have told no one about it anyway. Except for me, but no one ever takes anything I say for serious—except for Marty's dad, I guess, but that's for later. Ooter and me understood each other, even though he didn't really understand English, and I for sure didn't understand whatever language he was speaking. We just kind of knew what the other was trying to say.

Anyway, Ooter invited me over to dinner a while ago, after I had explained to him that, on account of us being best friends, we had to have dinner at each other's house. His mother, who was very nice to me, had cooked some German delicacy or something, but it tasted okay anyway. After dinner, Ooter gave me a tour of the house, and in his basement was the biggest and weirdest looking television set I've ever seen in my life. It took up an entire wall all by itself.

I could tell, just by looking at his face, that Ooter wasn't supposed to be playing with it. Now I didn't want to get him into trouble or anything, but I explained that, when you're still young, you're supposed to do silly things, so you can learn and grow up.

So Ooter went and turned on the television. But his dad had the Playboy channel or something hooked up, 'cause we only got this screen that wanted to know the password. There was a box full of symbols at the bottom of the screen, and we tried some of them randomly, but it didn't get us nowhere. It was getting late, and I had to go home, so I told Ooter to keep cracking at it. But by this time, Ooter was thinking that maybe we should forget about the whole thing. So I explained to him about the Playboy channel.

The next morning, at school, Ooter didn't look so good. What happened was he finally cracked the password. But instead of beautiful girls dancing in the nude, what he saw was this really ugly insect-monster like they have in old science-fiction movies. And this monster starts walking toward the screen, and Ooter races up the stairs and spills his guts to his parents.

But instead of getting angry, his father smiles and does nothing. And all of a sudden, this guy marches up the basement stairs and Ooter's parents tell him, "Say hello to your Uncle Bob, Ooter," or whatever, and it turns out that Uncle Bob brought his wife and two children with him.

Now I mentioned that Ooter was a little slow, but he knew something was wrong right away. So the next couple of days, he watched his parents real carefully. And he had more family members march up those basement stairs in the next few weeks than I care to count.

I decided never to go to Ooter's place for dinner after that first time, on account of my thinking that maybe his parents were on an exchange program and I for sure didn't want to end up in a world full of giant insects or anything. Ooter kept telling me all kinds of stories about how all these insect-things were coming through his dad's television screen and then turning into people. At that point was when I asked Ooter if we should inform the authorities, call 911 or something, but him and I agreed that it was too late for anything to be done and that no one would believe us anyway. Of course, by this time, Ooter had figured out that at least a good number of the authorities in town were really insect-things disguised as people, and they'd probably be pretty ticked if we ratted them out. Ooter knew exactly who was an insect-person, because his father kept meticulous records or something, so he could make up library cards and stuff for them.

So Ooter and I would discuss what we should do about it, like how we should stop the invasion, right? But we weren't no superkids or anything, and it's not like in the cartoons. "If it weren't for you darned kids, the invasion would have worked perfectly!" I once told Ooter, but he didn't get it. We'd get really excited talking about what we could do, but we never decided on any definite action or anything.

Some weeks passed, and Ooter was telling me who was an insect-thing on the inside and who wasn't. So when we had this new teacher come in, Ooter told me that the new teacher was an insect-thing. His name was Mr. Bellemont, and he was pretty nice, except that he gave us too much homework. And that he got really mad when we didn't do it.

And that he made us read this book called "My Teacher is An Alien" or something, which is not a funny thing as far as I'm concerned. They should be afraid or something, you know? But they go around, practically *telling* normal people that they're a bunch of insect-things.

Anyway, about a week ago, I convinced Ooter to talk to his parents about the whole thing. But I guess that didn't go so good, because he never spoke to me again. I mean, he'd just tell me to leave him alone and stuff, but I don't really care. Marty's my new best friend, and he's not big like Ooter, so the bullies started bothering me again, but at least *he* doesn't have insect-people coming out of his house, which is more than I can say for some people, right?

A couple of days ago, I told Marty about this whole thing, after making him promise to keep it a secret. I had to say something, on account of him being my best friend. But Marty broke his promise and told his dad. He invited me over to his house day before yesterday, which is when I found out that he had told his dad. So his dad asked me if I could name all the people I thought might be insect-people, and he promised me a dollar for every one I named, so I really put on my thinking cap. I named only eighteen or something, 'cause those were the only ones I was sure about, but his dad gave me a twenty anyway. Marty wasn't too happy about that, so his dad gave him twenty dollars too.

That night, I went and did all my homework. And I come to school the next day all happy, on account of having done all my homework. But there's this new teacher, and she starts talking about something completely different, so no one even checks that I did my homework, which makes a guy wish he never wasted his time doing his homework, you know?

And another thing that ticks me off is that Ooter's moved away or something, and he didn't even have the decency to say good-bye to me. He wasn't at school yesterday, and he's not here today. I called his house yesterday night, but no one picked up. So I dropped by, completely forgetting about the whole exchange program thing with the insect world. But it didn't matter. The driveway was empty, and I rang the bell till my hands dropped off, but no one answered.

Making Simbta

FOREWORD

Do you believe in soulmates?

I certainly do—but I believe you grow into soulmates together, not that another person is pre-made just for you. I believe the other person is actually a person in their own right: complex, unique, ever-growing and ever-changing; a complete individual, delightful and frustrating, mysterious and strange, full of surprises pleasant and otherwise.

The other notion, that of pre-existent soulmates (which is per-haps more prevalent than mine, and comes down to us from as far back as the ancient Greeks), is strange to me. Even if it's true that there exists someone who was custom-built to match you, what are the chances you'll grow up in the same city as this perfect mate? Or go to the same bar? Or meet on the same bus? With almost 7 billion people in the world, the vast majority of whom you'll never so much as hear about let alone encounter, what are the chances you'll meet "the One"? (Well, one in seven billion–assuming your soulmate was born around the same time as you and didn't die as a child–but that isn't the point).

I think defenders of this notion would say that it isn't a question of chance, it's a question of fate. If you believe that, though, what happens when your soulmate decides they don't want to be with you? That was the question on my mind when I sat down to write the next story.

S Ome people think that being a bartender is easy. Well I've done just about every job in the universe, legal and illegal, and I can tell you it's true: bartending really is easy. You pour drinks, you pretend to listen, you collect tips. You lean over to expose green flesh, you really collect tips—especially if, like me, you've got three boobs (four when I'm excited).

But bartending stops being easy when you start to care. That's the mistake I made with Q-ru.

He came in alone one night and I asked a question that I never would have asked anyone but a Polerian. "How's that pretty girl of yours?" I said.

The first rule of dealing successfully with clients is never be the first to bring up a relationship that might have gone south. But in my experience, Polerian relationships never went south.

Q-ru didn't say anything, but his ears started bleeding green.

"Oh, don't cry," I said, sitting down beside him. "Please don't cry."

"She's gone, far gone." He wouldn't even look at me. Twenty-seven eyes, tentacle-tethered around his head, and not a single one would meet mine.

"These things happen," I said.

Q-ru's eyes wobbled. "In the history of Polerians, never happened before, not once."

"You'll meet someone else," I said. By then, I should've known to check my assumptions and my clichés.

"No someone else," Q-ru said. "Q-ra is the one for Q-ru, Q-ru is the one for Q-ra. No someone else."

Finally I said something intelligent. "What happened?"

"Q-ra doesn't want to make simbta anymore, so no more simbta for us."

I nodded as if I followed. "Is that like making love?" I whispered.

"Physical act of reproduction?" Q-ru said, which was how his translator rendered my words. "No, of course not physical act of reproduction. Not talking about biological functions here but about simbta, about making simbta!"

"I'm sorry," I said, placing my hand on his shoulder. "I don't know what it means to make simbta."

"Making simbta is why we live," Q-ru said, calming down. "How we live is biological functions, why we live is to make simbta."

"Why doesn't she want to make simbta anymore?"

"Don't know. Why? Don't know. But Q-ra wants to be alone, all alone, and never make simbta again."

"Are you worried maybe she's making simbta with someone else?"

There are a few universal stares that don't require the use of a translator to understand. Q-ru looked at me like I was missing both brains.

"Not possible," he said. "Together, can make simbta. Apart, cannot make simbta. This is what Q-ra wants, apart, not making simbta."

"Wow, no more simbta," I said with wonder that was genuine even though I still had no idea what simbta was.

"No more simbta," Q-ru repeated. "Not for Q-ru."

I didn't know what else to say. Q-ru didn't want anything to drink, even at no charge. He left.

It wasn't hard to figure out why Q-ru had beamed into my bar. He'd been looking for some company away from other Polerians, who are a kind people unless you're a Polerian who can't make simbta, either because you haven't yet found your other (a few odd-balls) or because your other left you (in the history of the Polerians, Q-ru). He'd beamed into my bar for companionship and comfort, and I'd sent him on his way more depressed than when he'd arrived. That thought depressed me in turn, so much so that for the next few weeks I couldn't get my fourth breast to come out, no matter what I tried.

That's what happens when you stop pretending to listen and you start to actually care.

Time drags when you're waiting for something. I was waiting for Q-ru to come back. I tried to fill the hours sitting in front of my computer, digging through the omnipedia, learning as much as I could about the Polerians. But there just wasn't that much information out there. I found a few references to simbta, but no descriptions of what it might be. Later, I'd learn from Q-ru that as sacred as simbta is to the Polerians, they don't talk about it to outsiders. If not for his depression that one day, he may not have mentioned it to me at all.

Just the way it always happens, Q-ru beamed into my bar as I was about to give up on ever seeing him again. I wouldn't have thought it possible, but he looked even more depressed than before.

"Q-ru," I said. As much as I had wanted to see him again, now that he was there in front of me I wasn't sure what to say.

"Saying goodbye, that's all," Q-ru said. He looked at me with all his eyes; I blushed under that kind of attention.

"Goodbye?" I said, trying to make my voice sound light and playful. "You're-never-coming-into-this-bar-again goodbye or you're-taking-your-own-life goodbye?"

"Second goodbye. Taking-own-life goodbye."

"Q-ru, you can't do that!"

"Must do that," Q-ru said. "Nothing else to do but that."

"That's not true," I said.

"True, very true. For Polerians, not alive if not making simbta. As good as dead."

The pad on my apron beeped; someone was ordering a drink the table couldn't mix. I was working alone—the bartender I hire to help on busy nights hadn't shown up—but I ignored the beep anyway.

"Q-ru, give yourself time," I said. "Things will get better."

"Lots of time already. If continue to live, live only for the memory of the simbta Q-ra and Q-ru used to make, the simbta used to make but will never make, not ever again."

He reached for his arm-band. I did something I'd never done before for a customer who hadn't run up a tab. I hit my own band first and blocked his beam.

"Please," Q-ru said. "Came to say goodbye, said goodbye. Time to go now."

"Only if you promise not to kill yourself."

"Can walk out door."

Q-ru's big, but the bear at the back was bigger. "He won't kill you. But he'll hurt you. A lot."

"Please," Q-ru said, again.

I stood up. "Excuse me, I have to go mix exotic drinks for exotic customers."

Q-ru hung around until closing time, not drinking or eating, not talking to anyone. He sat at his table, looking more lonely than anyone I'd ever seen before. And working a bar, you see a lot of lonely people.

When everyone else was gone, I said to Q-ru, "Are you ready to promise, or will you be spending the night here?"

"Just want to go." His voice was full of so much sadness and despair, his twenty-seven eyes devoid of the merest spark of joy. "Why you care?" he said.

Why I care? I asked myself. Life is great just so long as you don't.

"Does anyone else care?"

Q-ru shook his eyes.

"Maybe that's why."

Amazingly, he smiled. "Not very good reason."

"I guess," I said, returning his playful smile. "But it's all I got."

"Lipka?" Q-ru said, turning to face me with his entire body for the first time that night.

With a nod, I typed the order into the table and removed the glasses when they filled up. I handed one to Q-ru, who emptied it in one gulp.

"Last drink," he said.

"But tradition insists on a last meal."

We hit the kitchen, cooking and eating through the night. Q-ru taught me a few Polerian recipes. I introduced him to celery. Although I'm a great cook, and I tried to show him a couple of fancy dishes, Q-ru was done when he came across the "green sticks." He spent the rest of the night crunching through stalk after stalk.

Q-ru didn't kill himself. I'd like to imagine that my friendship or some words of wisdom I imparted pulled him out of his suicidal depression, but I think the truth is that he really liked celery.

Q-ru couldn't return to his old job, surrounded by simbta-making Polerians, so I gave him work in my bar, with the rest of us simbta-less folk. It turned out Q-ru was a great cook himself, except for a bad habit he had of crossing off celery from my recipes.

He seemed happy enough, my customers liked his cooking, I liked his company (for years, my only permanent employee was the bear, who could only say three words—none of which I was interested in, no matter how many times he asked). Q-ru was happy. I was happy.

Then Q-ra beamed into my bar and turned everything upside-down.

A s much as I liked having Q-ru around, I wouldn't have begrudged him life with his one-true-love, making simbta and being happy. But I got the wrong hit off Q-ra, the second she materialized on my floor.

"Hello, Q-ra."

"Hello," she said. She employed all her eyes in a search for Q-ru, sparing none for me.

"Looking for someone?" I said.

"Q-ru."

"What makes you think he's here?"

Q-ra's eyes—all of them—focused on me, like a fleet of space-ships locking onto a target. "Know he's here."

I didn't remember Q-ra being that unpleasant. It made me wonder if the lack of simbta had changed her, or whether my perception was influenced by how much she had hurt Q-ru.

"Maybe you should just leave," I said, but I saw her eyes focus on something behind me and knew that Q-ru had come out of the kitchen.

Eavesdropping is horribly impolite, but I did it anyway and didn't try to hide that I was doing it. As a surprise for Q-ru, I'd been teaching myself a little Polerian. I didn't catch every nuance of the conversation, but I got the gist. She'd made the biggest mistake of her life, she wanted him back, she wanted them to make simbta again, forgive her, forgive her, forgive her.

"Q-ru, can I see you for a second?" I said, pulling him away. He let me lead him around, but most of his eyes were still on Q-ra.

"You have to say no."

"No," Q-ru said with a big smile.

"I'm not kidding around! You were ready to kill yourself over this girl. And now you're going to let her back into your life?"

"Yes."

"But she's all wrong for you."

"No," Q-ru said. "Only one who is right for me."

"You don't need her," I said, hurt at his words but not sure why.

There were lots of things I wanted to say, but I didn't say any of them. Q-ra's eyes started waving impatiently, and Q-ru looked like he might explode if he didn't get back to her.

I finally let him go, out of my grasp, out of my bar, out of my life. From the look Q-ra gave me as they left, pod-in-pod, I knew that she'd never let Q-ru see me again.

I should've given him more credit.

ONe night, just short of a year later, I asked my cook how things were going. Things were going fine, except that we were running out of celery. The customer at table E7 was ordering it by the stalk.

Startling several customers, I burst out of the kitchen. A Polerian sat at table E7, his back to me, but some of his eyes were looking into mine.

He stood. I ran over and threw my arms around him. Sometimes you don't realize how much you miss someone until you see them again.

"How are you, Q-ru?"

"Never better."

"And Q-ra?" I said. "Still freezing water with her warmth?"

Q-ru shrugged. "Don't know," he said. "Don't know, don't care."

"You're not together anymore?" I said, pulling away so I could look him in the face.

"Not together anymore. No."

"Since when?"

Since a few weeks ago.

I sat Q-ru down, pushed celery sticks toward him. "Start from the beginning."

Q-ru had wanted nothing more than to get back together with Q-ra. But once it happened—he wasn't happy. They were making simbta, just like all the other Polerians, but he wasn't happy. Q-ru couldn't explain it, but he didn't need to. I understood. Sometimes you don't realize how little you miss someone until you see them again.

She lost it when he told her he wanted a little time apart, maybe to travel the galaxy, to see how other people lived their lives, to meet new species and experience different cultures. She became desperate and ridiculed him publicly.

"To Q-ru's family. To Q-ru's friends. On the holos, everywhere. Q-ru no longer wants to make simbta, Q-ru's crazy. Crazy Q-ru."

He'd relented under all the pressure. For a while. But he wasn't happy and he could barely stand Q-ra. And a question weighed on his mind more than any other: why was simbta so great in the first place?

He mustered up the courage to leave. Q-ra said she never wanted to see him again; his family thought he was nuts; his friends were afraid to talk to him. But Q-ru had one final thing to do. Before leaving, he uploaded *The Simbta Spell (And How to Break Free)*, a book he'd spent most of the last year writing in secret. Within a few days, his book racked up more views than any other in the entire Polerian library.

"Well, aren't you a little revolution-starter?" I said, and Q-ru laughed and nodded with all his eyes.

I was the first stop on Q-ru's cross-galaxy vacation, paid for by the good Polerian readers.

"Once a month, Q-ru. That's how often I want you to visit."

"Can come with Q-ru," he said.

Of course I agreed; I used to be the greatest tour guide in the universe and Q-ru deserved (and could now easily afford) the best. No, really; that's the reason, and not because I wanted to spend as much time as possible with him.

Which is not to say that sometimes it's worth it, caring about others. For the last three weeks, no matter what I try, I can't get my fourth breast to retract. It's killer on my back.

And that's not the worst of it. A long time ago, I learned that the best way to live a happy life is to not care about anyone else, to not have your happiness depend on anyone but yourself. That's a hard ideal to live by when you're planet-hopping with a Polerian who's convinced himself he's in love with you. Especially when you're in love with him too.

At War

FOREWORD

How do you do the right thing when everyone around you is doing the wrong thing? At that point, with your single voice drowned out by the cacophony of everyone else's, is it even clear what is right anymore? Peer pressure is one of the strongest forces in the universe, and when your peers and everyone else around you seem like they're going off the rails, what do you do? It can often seem like you only have two options, neither of which is very desirable: do you abandon your own values and join the herd, maybe risk losing yourself but at least you've got lots of friends to make up for the loss? Or do you stay true to yourself, buck the trend, and end up alone?

Of course, there is a third option.

Y Ou weren't in the tent last night," Private Arthur Ritley said into his helmet's microphone.

From the other side of the wooden bridge, Private First Class Jean Trebaire turned to look at him but didn't answer.

Ritley kept walking. He only wanted to warn his partner. Wherever Trebaire was running off to (and really, in this forest in the middle of nothing, where was there to go?), he was bound to get caught.

"Have you told anyone?" Trebaire spoke very quietly; Ritley turned up the volume in his helmet's speakers.

"Of course not."

"You're planning to?"

Blackmail. Trebaire's mind had gone straight to blackmail. "I'm not planning to, no." Ritley's voice was dejected, worn-out.

They spent the next few hours in silence, guarding a bridge that probably wasn't even on the enemy's radar. Certainly it hadn't been used by the allies in weeks. There existed more direct routes to transport supplies and troops to the frontlines, routes not surrounded by a thick forest, routes that didn't involve crossing a wooden bridge thirty meters long, hanging above a chasm more than twenty kilometers deep. But someone somewhere up the chain of command had decided they wanted to hold the bridge and keep the surrounding area secure. So here they were.

That night, Ritley sat in his bed and watched (not for the first time) a message his wife had beamed him the night before. "I've been trying to be strong for you, baby," she said, her eyes avoiding the camera, nervous fingers toying with a silver hoop earring. "I'm sorry I couldn't hide it better... you're right. I am sad. I'm lonely, Arthur. You marry someone and you expect them... you expect not to be lonely all the time." She dropped her hand. "I know you're doing a good thing. I'm proud of you. But... this war could go on forever. What's to stop it? I don't know what I'm trying to say. I miss you a lot, that's all."

Ritley suddenly became aware that Trebaire was standing by his cot. He quickly turned off the screen, wondering how much of the message Trebaire had heard.

"About what you said this morning," Trebaire whispered. "Are you curious?"

Ritley looked around. Two soldiers were asleep on their cots at the other end of the large tent.

Of course he was curious. But he didn't want to get involved. "You're not supposed to leave camp, for any reason," Ritley whispered, staring up at the dark shadow of Trebaire's hulking frame.

"I want to show you. Come on."

Trebaire walked away, back to his own cot, without waiting to see if his partner would follow.

Ritley threw off his covers and got out of bed. From his footlocker, Trebaire pulled out a bundle of clothes. Ritley tried to focus his eyes, but it was hard to see; Trebaire hadn't turned on the small light above his cot.

"What am I looking at?" Ritley said, leaning down beside Trebaire.

Instead of answering, Trebaire unfolded the bundle to reveal a silvery object the size and shape of a slightly-too-tall, slightly-too-wide belt. Ritley had no idea what it was, and even in the relative darkness, his confusion must have shown on his face.

"PTD," Trebaire whispered, wrapping it up again but failing to replace it in the footlocker.

Ritley felt his stomach muscles tighten and immediately he regretted not following his initial instinct. He'd now crossed a threshold he couldn't uncross. If he kept quiet, he was an accomplice; if he said anything, he was a rat. Why had Trebaire shown him?

"Here's my advice to you," Ritley said. "Wherever and however you got that thing, destroy it right now."

He got up to leave, but Trebaire grabbed his arm and held him down. "Are you crazy? Don't you get it? I'm showing you because I'm willing to share."

"That's awfully generous." Ritley shook off Trebaire's hand. "But I'm not interested." He got up and went back to bed, half-expecting Trebaire to follow.

He didn't, and Ritley drifted off to sleep without having answered his wife's message for the second night in a row.

IT's illegal, that's why." Ritley knew they weren't supposed to chit-chat while on patrol, but everyone did because otherwise the boredom would drive you stir-crazy.

"You know where I was last night?" Trebaire said. "I went to this awesome comedy club in Montreal. This comedian starts going on about life on Mars, and how they think they're so much better than us. At least we can breathe *our* air. That's what he kept saying—at least on Earth we can breathe all by ourselves.

I've never laughed so hard. And the waitress—boobs like planets, man. Boobs like planets."

Ritley kicked a pebble at his feet. "I can go to all the comedy clubs in the world, when this war's over."

"Don't you miss your wife?"

Ritley didn't answer, but Trebaire didn't wait for him.

"I know you do. So go see her, you know? Strap on the belt, push a few buttons, and *boom!*—you're right there with her. Spend the night, come back in the morning."

Ritley pulled out a canteen and drank some water. To be with Tina again, even just for a little while, would be so amazing. He could hold her—just the thought made him happier than he'd been in a long time. Kiss her; feel close to her again. He didn't want to lose his wife. He didn't want to drift away and fade into a memory. Just a few hours.

But it wouldn't be right, would it? Jemke and Peterkowski didn't get to go home to their wives. The Master Corporal didn't get to go home to his wife. Why should he?

"I really wish I could," he said. "But it wouldn't be right." Trebaire snorted, but Ritley went on, "Besides, Personal Teleportation Devices were banned for a reason. They're not safe. I've seen videos of people dying from Meyer's Disease. It's not pretty." The images and sounds came back to him; dull cries for help as the drugged man's molecules disintegrated throughout his body, while solemn-looking doctors stood by helplessly.

"Meyer's is a myth, a conspiracy to keep teleportation out of civilian hands," Trebaire said. "And even if Meyer's is real, you really think a soldier should be making long-term health plans?"

Ritley shook his head. Where had Trebaire gotten the thing, any—

He brought his rifle to his shoulder and pointed it at a large tree a few meters to his left. "Trebaire, I may have something." It was deathly quiet as Ritley approached the tree and—very slowly—circled around it. Nothing. He looked up, pointed his gun at the rich foliage of the tree.

The leaves shook a little. Or was that his imagination? Ritley's finger tightened around the trigger. He watched, heart thudding in his chest. Suddenly a black blur exploded from the sky and Ritley fired.

Trebaire joined him, and in a few moments so did the rest of the squad, including the Master Corporal, responding to the alarm sent through camp when Ritley discharged his gun. They formed a circle around the mutilated, charred bird corpse.

"I thought I heard a noise," Ritley said, trying to hide his embarrassment.

The Master Corporal nodded once, then sent out the teams to sweep the area. Ritley wondered if the Master Corporal really believed there might be something or someone to find, or if he just wanted to help Ritley save face. Either way, he was grateful.

Ritley and Trebaire swept their area in complete silence, even though Ritley was dying to say, "See? What would happen if the alarm goes up while you're sipping martinis in some night club in San Francisco?" But he kept quiet and they cleared their area without incident, as did the other teams.

Dinner consisted of more potatoes—cubed this time, with garlic and parsley—and some strips of beef. The Master Corporal ate with the rest of the squad, which was something he almost never did. Ritley had caused some excitement today; even a false alarm was enough to send a burst of energy through camp.

After dinner, Ritley headed for his cot, desperate to record a message for his wife, a message so full of sympathy and understanding and love and humor that it would make everything okay. But Trebaire followed him into the tent, and sat on the ground near his bed.

"Want to borrow it tonight?" Trebaire's voice was so soft Ritley had to lean in to hear him.

"I already told you, no."

"You're serious? You're really going to pass this up?"

Peterkowski walked past and looked at them curiously.

"Where'd you get it, anyway?" Ritley said, when Peterkowski was gone.

"All right," Trebaire said, after a moment. "All right, I'll tell you. We're partners, right?"

Ritley nodded.

"About a year ago, I was on patrol with another guy, guarding a base in Eagle Pass. It was completely quiet—sort of like here, you know? One day, my partner and I suddenly found ourselves staring at these six Mexican guys, materializing in front of us. They looked startled—I don't think in front of our base is where they meant to teleport. We killed all six before they could aim their guns at us."

"That's impossible," Ritley blurted out.

Trebaire gave a short, derisive laugh. "Why? Because teleportation is illegal? You really have no clue, do you? Have you heard anything about this? Have you heard about four of our enemies teleporting into one of our camps? You know why you haven't? Because our side is probably doing the same thing. I bet there's a troop in our army somewhere that's specially trained to fight using PTDs."

Ritley hadn't missed the glint in Trebaire's eyes as he spoke. "What do you mean, four enemies?"

Trebaire shrugged, then his face split into a grin again.

Once more Ritley regretted having asked his questions. He didn't want to be party to any of this. He just wanted to finish his tour and go home. He wanted to keep his nose clean.

"I've shared a lot with you, haven't I?" Trebaire said.

"Look, keep using the belt yourself. I don't want to." Trebaire's angry, frustrated look made Ritley want to say more. "Forget about only putting yourself at risk. Remember that child in Des Moines? A guy teleported beside him, half his arm materializing in the child's head. The kid didn't die right away."

The look of anger on Trebaire's face didn't fade. "You want to keep yourself innocent, is that it? So you can rat me out whenever you want?"

Ritley drew back. "No, that's not it at—"

"Listen to me, okay? By next week, every one of these guys and gals will have spent a night with their boyfriend or girlfriend or wife or hooker or whatever. Okay? And no matter how much you beg, you've lost your chance."

He got up and stormed away before Ritley could say anything else.

TRebaire was true to his word. He revealed his secret to the squad (minus the commanding officers) and one by one they took him up on the offer to share his belt.

Dinner conversations turned from the war and memories of home to memories of the night before. Peterkowski watched four movies in a row in a theater in his hometown of Sudbury. Brontel's husband was so shocked when she stepped into their bedroom that he couldn't speak for a full five minutes.

Ritley stayed quiet during these conversations. He wondered what the others thought of that. He wondered if Trebaire told them he'd refused to try the belt.

He wanted to laugh along with their funny stories, and smile as they shared their excited plans for their next turn with the belt, but he found it hard to summon the energy. He was indignant, to begin with. They were breaking the law and they were bound to get caught—what if Brontel's husband bragged to someone at work? Even worse, they were putting their lives and the lives of others in danger. But besides all that, Ritley knew there was another reason he couldn't share in their stories—he was jealous. Was it fair that Brontel got to see her husband? Was it fair that they didn't worry about the risks—to themselves, to others? Was it fair that they lived with quiet consciences?

And not just jealous. Left out. He couldn't add to the conversation. He didn't have any stories of his own to share. He spent the night at camp. He hadn't gone to a fireworks display in Prince Edward Island, or to play poker in Vegas.

He knew Trebaire wouldn't offer sympathetic ears, but one day on patrol, he couldn't stop himself from saying, "So we've all really taken to teleportation, huh?"

Trebaire took his time before responding. "Yup, I guess we have."

"No one else is too worried about Meyer's, I guess."

"I guess."

Ritley still felt horrible. Outside looking in, isolated and alone. "Or that the Master Corporal is stuck here, day after day."

"Nope. I guess they just mind their own business."

"Yeah." Ritley felt an almost overwhelming urge to ask—beg, if he had to—Trebaire for a turn after all. Just once, just long enough to run his fingers through his wife's hair and tell her how much he missed her. But he kept his mouth shut.

After a few minutes of awkward, tense silence, Trebaire said, "Listen, man...I've been a jerk, okay? If you want your turn with the belt, you can have it. Okay?"

Okay! Ritley screamed in his head. *Okay!*

But he couldn't bring himself to voice the thought. Why should something stop being wrong just because more people are doing it? And even more—he hated admitting this to himself—even more, he didn't want to sink to Trebaire's level. So much for noble morality; his overriding thought was that he didn't want Trebaire to break through him, to have won.

"Still not interested," he said, then waited for Trebaire's angry invectives.

No reply; not even a snort. Ritley wondered about Trebaire's restraint—until later that night, when he realized that his partner had spent the time planning.

Ritley jumped out of bed—or tried to. Strong hands held him down while someone shoved a gag into his mouth and someone else tied his hands together. Jemke's face floated into sight, holding a piece of cloth. Ritley kicked at him, missed, and his view went black as the fabric covered his eyes.

They dragged him out of bed, then walked perhaps three or four kilometers before coming to a stop. They removed the blindfold and Ritley found himself facing Trebaire in an open clearing in the forest. The other soldiers formed a circle around the two partners. Trebaire and the others had their guns drawn.

"Are you afraid to die, Private Ritley?" Trebaire said. "That's what happens to rats. We exterminate them."

"There are worse things than dying, Private First Class Trebaire. But I'm no rat."

Trebaire faced the circle of soldiers, like a lawyer in a courtroom. "I've said this to you all in private, but now I say it in the open, in front of the rat himself. Today while on patrol, Private Ritley told me that he disapproved of our use of the PTD belt. Private Ritley squeaks when he walks, and never did an illegal act in his whole life. And he doesn't want us to either. He said that if we didn't stop using the belt immediately, he'd go straight to the Master Corporal and report each and every one of us."

They waited, but Ritley didn't respond.

Brontel cleared her throat. "Well, is it true?"

"It's true that I disapprove," Ritley said. "It's not true that I'm planning on ratting anyone out."

Trebaire laughed. "We believe you, Ritley. We'll take your word for it, forget all about what you told me today."

"You're a liar," Ritley said, matter-of-factly. "And by morning I may be dead, but you'll still be a liar."

Ritley had never seen Trebaire look so ugly before. In the moonlight, his face seemed to glow with hatred and anger.

"It's up to you," Trebaire said, speaking to the soldiers. "We can all stop using the PTD belt. Or we can put a bullet in this would-be rat and call it a night."

"Will you promise to take your turn on the belt?" It was Peterkowski this time.

"I wish I could. But I can't."

"Why not?"

"Because I know it's wrong."

"Why is it so wrong?" Peterkowski said, visibly uncomfortable with his sudden nomination as spokesperson for the group.

Ritley shrugged. What could he tell them that they didn't already know? "Because I feel in my gut that using the belt is wrong," he said. "So I can't."

Trebaire punched him in the stomach, dropping Ritley to his knees. He pressed his gun to Ritley's forehead. "Last chance to save your life."

Ritley closed his eyes and prepared to die. *I love you, honey*, he said to his wife, hoping that somehow she'd hear.

But Trebaire's grunt made him open his eyes. Peterkowski had pushed Trebaire away from him.

"We were only trying to scare you," Peterkowski said, bending down to untie Ritley's hands and helping him up. "So you wouldn't rat us out." He looked away for an instant, then met Rit-ley's eyes again. "I'm sorry."

Trebaire didn't resist when Peterkowski reached for his gun. "Not that Ritley can't take care of himself in a fist fight," he said to Trebaire, "but do anything stupid and I'll rat you out myself and make sure you spend the rest of your life in prison, okay?"

He turned away and headed back to camp and, one by one, the other soldiers did as well, leaving Trebaire and Ritley standing alone in the clearing.

"You think you've won, don't you?" Trebaire shoved his face into Ritley's. "You haven't won. Tomorrow they'll be begging me for their turn at the belt. They'll forget all about your false heroics. They don't want to be heroes, get it? They just want their turn, that's all."

"I think you should request a new partner," Ritley said, turning away from him and heading back to camp.

Trebaire didn't follow. "Yeah, I'll request a new partner all right. I'll tell them you're a chatty little schoolgirl. Can't concen-trate on my patrols, you know? Hey Ritley, you hear what I'm saying to you? You haven't won!"

Ritley walked back to camp. For a while, Trebaire's strained voice accompanied him, screaming that Ritley hadn't won, until it faded away, replaced by the soft, quiet sounds of the sleeping forest.

R itley played back his wife's latest message again. Staring into the camera with her big brown eyes, she told him to be strong, that he wasn't alone because she'd always be there for him, and that she missed seeing his smile. "They haven't made you forget how to smile, have they?"

He opened a new message and pushed the button to start a recording.

"OK, you got me." He shrugged. "To be honest, I can't even remember why they bothered me so much. I'll tell you the whole story when I get home… it's pretty much over now, I think.

"Honey, thank you for your messages. Really. And thanks for not pushing me for details just yet."

Ritley shook his head. "You know, we've spent so much time lately talking about me. I want to hear about you and what's going on in your end of the world."

He touched the button to stop recording. He stared at the last frame of his message, his smiling face frozen on the screen. Then, nodding, he pushed the button to transmit the message to his wife.

The Curious Case of the Book Baron

FOREWORD

The love of reading and the love of books are related, but they're not quite the same thing.

Many of my stories, including the ones in this collection, were first published in web-based magazines. When I was starting out as a writer, though, a large majority of established authors looked down their noses at ebooks and didn't consider them "real" publications or valid credits. Of course, the world has changed: in the summer of 2010, Amazon started selling more ebooks than paper-based books, a trend that continues to favor electronic print over paper print with no sign of slowing down. Now those established authors are scrambling to have as many of their short stories and backlist novels up for sale on various ebook platforms, because—increasingly—that's where the audience is, and so, that's where the money is.

From the first, though, I knew that to be read is to be read, whether your words were being read on paper or on screen. And for those of us who love to read—to be entertained, to learn something, to encounter interesting characters and be transported to new worlds–ebooks serve the purpose just as well, and in some ways far better, than paper books.

Will paper books die, as many book-lovers fear? I think it's safe to say that as long as there are book-lovers around at all (people who treat books as objects of art, to be displayed in their homes; as expressions of their values and interests; as conversation-pieces—let alone people who love the smell and feel of a paper-bound book), the answer is no.

And although ebooks were not at all on my mind when I wrote "The Curious Case of the Book Baron," I think the story demonstrates at least one other advantage paper books can have over ebooks.

THE alarm clock rang. Diego reached out to snooze it, but something was in the way, something hard and blocky. He opened his eyes, then cursed.

He picked up the phone behind the alarm clock and dialed Natalie's number.

"Hello?"

"He got me," he said. "The bastard got me."

"Which book is it?" Natalie said.

"What? Who cares?"

"I'm curious."

With his free hand, he picked up the book and held it up to the light that filtered in through the window's blinds. *"Ben-Hur,"* he said. "By Lew Wallace."

"Like the movie?"

"You're missing the point, Natalie. The bastard broke into my house—*my* house."

Natalie didn't say anything.

"Meet me at the station house in half-an-hour, OK?"

"OK," Natalie said. "Bring the book."

Diego checked his apartment door and then the building doors but couldn't find any signs of forced entry. *He picked the locks,* Diego thought. *Or he has a key.*

As he walked outside to his car, Diego thought through the list of people who had a key to his place: the landlord; Pieter, who came by to clean once a week; his mom. No one else.

Maybe it's Mom, Diego thought with a sigh. *Maybe she's the one behind all this.*

A T his desk on the second floor of the station house, Diego flipped through the confiscated books. All were in pristine condition; DNA and fingerprint analysis came up with nothing— not even the DNA and fingerprints of the victims. And none of the books had any markings or dedications that might provide leads.

Natalie tilted her head to look at him from behind her computer screen. "The newspapers are calling him the Book Baron."

"Are they now?"

"Don't be cross."

"We're never going to catch this guy," Diego said, rolling his chair around the desk so he could face Natalie. "He's so confident he even broke into my house. A detective's house!"

"You'll catch him," Natalie said absentmindedly. She had gone back to reading the news on her screen.

"Maybe we should call in one of those psychics."

Natalie looked at him. "Wow, you really are desperate."

"He broke into my house, Nat. Right under my nose. And I slept right through it. The guy's mocking me."

"You'll get him," she said again.

Diego nodded half-heartedly, then rolled himself back to his desk, back to the boxful of books, back to the form on his computer monitor that listed the clues for this case. There weren't many.

W Hen he got home that night, there was a letter waiting for him on the nightstand where the book had been. He opened the envelope and read:

> *Dear Detective Montel,*
>
> *I have worked hard to put books into the homes of the good people of our city. You've taken a few away—all the ones you've been made aware of, I know; but some people don't call the police when someone leaves a gift in their home. Now that you know the books are useless as evidence, though, I'd like for you to give them back, please. Books shouldn't be in a cardboard*

box on some police station's laminate floor. Books should be in people's homes and in their hands.

Thank you in advance for your cooperation.

Your Friend,

The Book Baron.

The letter was computer-printed, but that was fine by Diego.

He was on the phone as soon as he finished reading it. "I need to send a letter to the lab. I want the works. I want to know *everything* about this letter."

He called Natalie next. "He made his first mistake, Nat. We've got him!"

It didn't work out that way. About a week later, a technician from the lab hand-delivered the report to Diego. That was unusual enough; even more unusual was the look the technician gave him.

"What?" Diego said.

"Is this a joke?" the technician said. "Or some kind of test?"

"What?"

"We tested the letter like you asked. The ink came from a LaserBuddy 4000."

Diego had a LaserBuddy 4000; it sat on a wheeled cabinet beside his desk.

"And the paper is twenty-pound white, manufactured by Cromtar."

Twenty-pound white paper, manufactured by Cromtar was department-issue. An opened stack lay on a shelf beneath the LaserBuddy.

The technician wasn't finished, but Diego ignored him and turned to his computer. He brought up the printer logs and studied them. At first nothing odd jumped out at him. But then he saw it: a single page, sent to the printer at 8 P.M. about a week before by someone logged in using the guest account.

"He used my printer," Diego said, interrupting the technician and whatever he was saying. "He sat in my chair and typed on my keyboard. The nerve!"

"Detective?" the technician said. "You're saying the Book Baron was here, in this precinct?" There was a smile playing on his face.

Diego ripped the envelope out of his hands. "Thanks for the report."

The technician didn't leave right away. When he finally did, Diego stood to see Natalie over her monitor. She was staring at the screen in seemingly deep concentration, but her lips had disappeared into her mouth, as if she might explode into laughter without this precaution.

"Even you, Nat?" he said. "Even you aren't taking me seriously?"

She met his eyes with her own—beautiful brown eyes, Diego thought suddenly, like a teddy bear's. But her lips escaped into a smile and, unable to stop herself, she started to tremble with laughter.

Diego fell back in his seat. "I guess I'm the only one who thinks b-and-e is a serious offense, huh?"

"Oh, please," Natalie said, still hidden behind her computer monitor.

"What if he took something?" Diego said, raising his voice. "A little trade, jewelery for a paperback."

"No one reported theft. Not even you."

He could tell from her voice that she was still smiling.

"I haven't finished checking over my house," Diego said. "And if he so much as breathed on me, that could be home invasion."

Natalie laughed out loud this time.

Diego smiled, then laughed a little himself. "Fine," he said. "Trespassing—that's serious enough, isn't it?"

"Wait a minute," Natalie said, feigning seriousness. "He used your computer, your printer, your ink. Maybe you can make a case for burglary after all. Let's see—if you add up the unlawful use of electricity, paper, and ink, you come up to a quarter easily."

"Funny," Diego said. "Very funny."

Over the next few days, Diego asked around—on his floor, on the ground floor, on other floors; he even asked the hotdog vendor outside—but no one could remember seeing anything suspicious. He traced the names from the visitor logs, but they were all accounted for. However he'd gotten into the building, the Book Baron hadn't signed in at the front desk.

By then, the reports had stopped coming in. Not that the Book Baron had stopped operations, Diego knew. But as his fame grew, people weren't as freaked out that a stranger had been in their home. The last time Diego did a canvass, more than one person asked him if he had nothing better to do, or if the city had run out of real criminals.

What if next time he leaves you a bomb instead of a book? Diego thought, but he didn't say anything.

IT's better than the movie," Natalie said, holding out the copy of *Ben-Hur* that had appeared on his nightstand.

Diego looked up at her, but didn't take the offered book. "You read it?"

"I was bored."

Diego ripped the book from her hand. "This box," he said, returning the paperback, "is not your personal lending library."

"What's the big deal?" Natalie said, returning to her desk.

Diego followed her. "The big deal? You're reading his books. You're encouraging him!"

"I won't tell him I read it," Natalie said. "If you won't tell either, then he won't know and he won't feel encouraged. OK?"

Diego didn't say anything.

"Besides," Natalie said. "It's a really good book. You should read it."

Diego closed his eyes. "Do you know that I had to beg the lab to analyze the books? The Property Room wouldn't even look at them, let alone store them. The lieutenant growls whenever he sees me working this case."

Natalie stood and placed a hand on his shoulder; he opened his eyes. She smelled very nice today, Diego couldn't help but notice. "Maybe you should just return the books. He's harmless."

"If I return the books," Diego said, "then he wins. Besides—" He stopped, was quiet for a moment. A thought had occurred to him, was even now crystallizing in his mind. He continued, speaking slowly, "Besides, I can't stand not figuring things out."

"What is it?" Natalie said.

Diego turned to look at his desk, then looked back at Natalie, then looked again at his desk.

"What?" she said. She placed her head beside his, to look at the desk the way he was seeing it.

Man, her hair smells amazing, Diego thought. He told himself to focus. "How did he know?" he said.

"What?"

Diego walked back to his desk. "How did he know I keep the books in a box underneath my desk?"

"What do you mean?" Natalie said. "He was right here. He used your computer."

"No," Diego said. "No." He bent over and pushed the box all the way to the back of the desk. "I do that every night," he said to Natalie. "Pieter goes crazy if I leave stuff in his path, so I make sure I push it all the way."

Natalie opened her mouth, but Diego shook his head slowly. Whenever he mentioned Pieter, Natalie felt the need to lecture Diego. He was lazy for not cleaning his own house; and he was doubly lazy for not finding his own cleaning service but offering the job to the janitor at work.

Natalie shrugged innocently and closed her mouth.

Diego stood, walked away from his desk, then turned to look at it. He bent his knees, sinking lower. He walked back, ignoring the looks from the other detectives and keeping his gaze fixed on the desk. He sat in his chair, rolled away a few feet.

"No way," he said to Natalie. "Even if he sees the box, it's just a stretch of cardboard, right? Who would notice the presence of a cardboard box underneath a desk, pushed all the way to the back?"

"You're reaching," Natalie said; only then did Diego notice that she had positioned herself between him and the lieutenant's office window; she didn't want the lieutenant to suspect Diego was still working the case.

That thought, and her words, deflated Diego's expanding enthusiasm. "What else have I got?" he said.

He'd been looking down; when Natalie didn't answer, he looked up. The lieutenant was standing in front of his desk.

"Where are the books?" the lieutenant said.

"What books?" Diego said, and Natalie gave him a cross look before she returned to her desk. He'd promised her he'd be more respectful of the lieutenant; it was just so hard to do when the fat man was in front of him.

The lieutenant placed his stubby-fingered hands on Diego's desk. "The books from the Book Baron case, Detective," he said, speaking slowly.

"Oh, those books," Diego said. "I've got them right here. Why?"

The lieutenant smiled an ugly grin that revealed his smoke-stained teeth. "Time to give them back."

"What?" Diego said.

"The media is calling us the Grinch," the lieutenant said.

"Who cares?"

"The captain does. And so do I. People have been phoning my office, asking for the return of their books. They've become something of a collectible, I suppose; it's cool to get one, and these people want theirs back." The lieutenant's smile faded, and he pulled his hands off Diego's desk. "Look, I know you want to solve this. But I can't have you spending time on the case anymore. It doesn't look good."

Diego nodded. "Yes, I understand."

When the lieutenant had left, Diego walked around to Natalie's desk and knelt beside her. "I figured it out," he said, whispering.

"Figured what out?" Natalie spoke softly, too.

"The Book Baron," Diego said. "While that gasbag"—with his nose, he pointed at the lieutenant's office—"was yakking, I figured out who it is."

"Who is it?"

"Pieter."

"Pieter. Really."

Diego nodded. "Who else would notice a cardboard box under-neath my desk, that wasn't there before? He would, right? Maybe his mop hit up against it while he was cleaning. Who else is up here after everyone has left? He walks in—raising zero suspicion because he's supposed to be here—and uses my computer."

Diego's knees started burning; he stood up. When Natalie didn't move, but kept staring at him, he motioned for her to join him. Almost reluctantly, she pushed her chair away from the desk and stood up, then followed him into the hallway.

Making sure no one was around to eavesdrop, he said, "So what do you think, Nat?"

"Well, Pieter does have a key to your apartment," she said, "because you're too lazy to clean your own house."

"It's not laziness," Diego said, rolling his eyes. "It's helping a friend from high school supplement his income, that's all."

Natalie nodded in an exaggerated way, as if she wouldn't dream of disagreeing with him.

Diego waved his hands, as if to wave away the topic. "So you agree with me about Pieter?"

"I didn't say that."

Diego felt his shoulders fall as his gaze dropped to the ground. Was she still not taking him seriously?

"But there's no harm in having a chat with him, right?"

Diego looked back at her. He smiled, then he nodded.

H<small>I</small>, Diego."
Diego turned around. Pieter was standing in the doorway. He wore a pair of blue jeans paint-stained with splotches of faded white and an old T-shirt. He didn't look like the baron of anything.

"Pieter," Diego said, standing up. "Thanks for stopping by."

"I only have fifteen minutes before my shift starts."

"Right in there," Diego said, motioning toward an interview room. "And don't worry, this shouldn't take long."

"If this is about the Book Baron, I still don't remember seeing anyone suspicious milling around here."

"That's okay, I'd still like to speak with you."

He followed Pieter into the room; they both sat down. Car sounds drifted in through an open window at the back. Diego sat quietly; he didn't look at Pieter, as if the other man wasn't even in the room, and listened to the city sounds.

"Were you lonely, Diego?" Pieter said finally. "Or did you call me in here for a reason?"

Diego leaned forward, placing his arms on the table between them. "Did you put a copy of *Ben-Hur* in my room?"

Pieter nodded.

For a moment, Diego thought Pieter had misunderstood the question. "You did?"

"Yes."

"So you're the Book Baron?"

"No," Pieter said. "Not really."

Diego stared at him. "You want to explain that to me?"

"Did you read the book?"

Diego shook his head.

"I'm sorry to hear that," Pieter said.

"Tell me about the Book Baron, Pieter."

"He doesn't exist," Pieter said. "He's a bunch of people."

Diego waited.

"It started with my writer's group," Pieter said.

"You're still writing after all these years?"

"Yeah." There was a slightly awkward, protracted pause. "Anyway, some writer friends of mine and I get together once a week and we critique each other's stories. And we talk, of course—about sales and good reviews, about rejections, about different theories and techniques, about what's happening in the world—about everything, really."

"What does this have to do with the Book Baron?"

"At one of these meetings, I mentioned that I was at someone's house, cleaning, when I realized that that person didn't own a single book. This person didn't have a bookshelf—he'd never read a book so good that he wanted to hold onto it, let alone two or three. Maybe he'd never read a book outside of school."

"So?"

"It's depressing. A house without books; it's like a person without a soul. It just shouldn't happen, you know?"

In his mind, Diego saw the pieces lift up, as if by a gust of wind, and fall into place. "So you decided to force books into people's homes, whether they want them or not?"

Pieter shook his head, but he didn't seem offended. Diego had tried to push him a little, but without effect.

Pieter said, "When I told my friends how depressed that house had made me, they said, 'So why not give him a book as a gift?' But it's not about possession; it's about enjoying and cherishing the books. If I give someone a book, they say thanks and maybe they never look past the cover. The question I asked was: How do I get him to give the book a chance?"

Pieter leaned forward and smiled like a child who has solved a difficult math problem. "What if a book just showed up in your house? You have no idea who put it there or why—one day, it just appears. Would you read it?"

As if realizing something too late, Pieter lost his smile and sat back in the chair. "I guess in your case we know the answer. But my theory was, you'd read the book. You'd give it a chance. And that's all I wanted." Pieter shrugged. "Anyway, the next time I was over cleaning, I left him a book."

Diego suddenly realized something. "So you didn't sneak into my house?"

Pieter's eyebrows drew together and his chin disappeared into his neck as his head tilted down in confusion.

"When did you leave the book on my nightstand?" Diego said.

"When I cleaned. Thursday." Pieter's lips stretched into a smile as realization flooded his face. "You didn't notice it until the next morning! You thought I snuck into your room in the middle of the night?"

"I was tired Thursday night; it was dark and. . . ." Diego closed his mouth, then couldn't help but smile. "Pretty observant for a detective, huh?"

"If ever I kill someone," Pieter said, "I've got the perfect place to hide the body."

Diego's smile faded. "You're very funny for a guy who could be in serious trouble, Pieter. You wasted"—he ticked them off on his fingers—"my time, the lab's time, my partner's time, my lieutenant's time, the—"

Pieter's look made Diego stop speaking. Of course it was stupid; what charges could he bring against him? Making a detective look silly?

"It's odd, isn't it?" Pieter said. "I never imagined people would go to the cops after finding a book in their house. Were they afraid the Gideons were branching out, in technique and subject matter, and wanted to stop the invasion before it was too late?"

"No," Diego said. "But they didn't like the idea that someone—a stranger—had been in their home."

"Until more people reported the same thing."

"Yeah. Then it became like being chosen by Santa Claus."

Pieter checked his watch.

"Just one more thing," Diego said. "Why didn't we find any fingerprints on the books?"

"I don't know, D," Pieter said, using Diego's nickname from high school and shrugging in an exaggerated way. "But I suppose it's possible someone may have given them all a quick wipe-down."

"You think that's funny? Ever heard of tampering with evidence!"

"Oh, come on," Pieter said. "It was meant as a joke, to tease you. I was wondering how long it would take you to figure things out. Besides, what kind of evidence is kept in a cardboard box underneath a desk?"

"It's those farts in the Property Room, they wouldn't even...." Diego's voice lowered and then he stopped talking, like a wind-up toy winding down. Why was he trying to pin something on Pieter, anyway? Was it his wounded ego looking for retribution?

"If I was serious about hiding my involvement in this, Detective," Pieter said, speaking slowly, "I think I could do a better job than walking in here, only too happy to tell you the truth."

"You're right; I'm sorry. You've been one-hundred percent cooperative and I appreciate that. OK?"

Pieter's shoulders dropped as he relaxed. He nodded.

"Good," Diego said. "Just one more thing, for real this time. You said that the Book Baron is a lot of people."

"Yeah. I certainly didn't give away all those books all by my-self. When I told my writer's group what I'd done, they started leaving behind some of their favorite books—in a friend's home, on a coworker's desk, even on the bus or a table at a café. But you want to know the most amazing thing?"

"What?"

"We stopped placing books several weeks ago. But there are still reports of the Book Baron striking—which means that others have picked up the idea and are running with it."

"Sounds like a virus to me," Diego said.

Pieter stood up. "I'm already late."

"Thanks for your time, Pieter."

"No problem." He moved toward the door, then turned around. "If you're not going to enjoy the book, give it to someone who will."

Pieter was out the door before Diego could respond.

Natalie stood beside his desk, holding a small paperback in her hand. "Did you do this?" she said.

"Did I do what?" It was hard not to smile, but he managed.

Natalie's head tilted to one side; she always did that when she suspected someone wasn't being honest with her. "I found this book on my chair," she said. "Did you put it there?"

"What's the book?"

She held it up.

"*The Catcher in the Rye*," he read. "Good book."

"Is that a confession?"

"No."

"You're a horrible liar, Diego," she said. "Just admit it so I can thank you."

"Yeah, it was me," he said, finally smiling. He pointed a finger at the novel. "That's one of my favorite books from high school. In fact," he added, with an almost apologetic lift of his shoulders, "it's the only book I read in high school."

"Well, thank you for it," Natalie said.

"You're welcome."

She started to walk away, then stopped and turned back. "You've never given me anything before."

Diego stared at her. Was it his imagination, or did she look nervous?

"Maybe I can treat you to dinner," she said. "I mean, like a real dinner; at a sit-down restaurant, I mean."

If it was hard to keep from smiling before, it was impossible now. "OK," he said. "Yeah, that sounds good."

"OK," Natalie said. She was smiling too.

When she was sitting at her desk again, hidden by her computer monitor, Diego whispered, "I always knew you had a crush on me."

For a moment, he thought she hadn't heard. But then she whispered back: "You're such a child, Diego." A pause, and then, "Are you free tonight?"

"Well, I had planned to finish that brick the Book Baron left for me," Diego said, still whispering. "But I'll change my plans for you, Nat."

Out of the corner of his eye, Diego saw the lieutenant approaching.

"What are you two whispering about?" he said, standing between them.

"Nothing," Diego said. "Certainly not about you." Diego didn't know if Natalie had smiled at that. *Probably not*, he thought.

The lieutenant gave Diego a dirty look, then stomped back to his office.

"Soon as I'm done with it, I'm passing *Ben-Hur* to the lieutenant," Diego said. "He'll just love Messala."

Natalie laughed out loud, a quick, snort-like sound he'd never heard her make before.

A Story of Fear, Faith, and Love

Chasing Carrots

IN the introduction to his self-proclaimed final novel, George Han wrote: "I've spent my whole life chasing carrots. I'm not going to do that anymore."

Canada's greatest literary voice had burned out after only three books. Although this country has never been expert at encouraging its literary children, the nation seemed to make an exception in Han's case. His first novel, published without fanfare by a small press in Saskatchewan, won the Governor General's Award for Fiction and became a national bestseller (in Canada, though, a book that sells half-a-dozen thousand copies is hailed as a bestseller); his second novel won the Trillium Book Award (and, incidentally, spent fifty-six weeks on the New York Times Bestseller List). Although it sold very well, his third novel won nothing at all, likely because Han declared that he refused, in advance, any and all awards. Reviewers of that third novel blasted Han, for the book and for his proclamation, which they saw as presumptuous and arrogant.

In the years since I read Han's introduction to that final novel—especially those mysterious words of farewell—I'd often wondered why Han had stopped writing and how an artist of his genius could silence so much creativity. A singer sings, a painter paints, a writer writes. But George Han—*the* writer, as far as my youth was concerned—wasn't writing anymore.

Han wanted his privacy, and a slighted literary establishment and an easily-distracted media were only too happy to oblige. He melted away into the kind of obscurity that would have made J.D.

Salinger burn with envy.

So little was known of Han by the time I decided to write an article about him that no one could say for certain if he were alive or dead. I placed some calls and called in some favors, and soon I had a phone number and address for Han—alive and well and collecting royalties and filing income tax returns.

I dialed the number. On the third ring, a woman answered, out of breath but perfectly lovely and pleasant nonetheless.

I asked if this was George Han's residence. Yes, it was. George Han the writer? Yes. I explained who I was and what I wanted.

"No problem," she said, perfectly lovely and perfectly pleasant. "When would you like to come by?"

"How about tomorrow?" Anxious as I was to meet Han, I made the request only half-seriously, and perhaps to soften her up for a meeting sooner than she might otherwise accept.

"Sure," she said.

"Wow," I said and she laughed delightfully.

The doubts set in during the hour-long plane ride from Toronto to Ottawa. What if Han himself refused to see me? What if he were truly washed up, not only not writing but not thinking or not really living either?

I'd been galvanized by the prospect of meeting my favorite writer and shedding light on a lifelong mystery. But standing underneath the concrete bridge outside of the arrivals section of the International Airport, I was paralyzed by the thought that maybe it was better if the world, and me with it, never found out what had become of George Han.

But if I returned without an interview, I reasoned, I couldn't claim the cost of the plane ticket. And I'd look like a fool. And I'd always regret it. And besides, for better or worse, I *wanted* to know what had become of George Han.

I got into a cab and gave the driver the address. Despite my fears about what I would find when I met Han, or maybe because of them, I couldn't stop my hands from shaking. It was as if I'd erased the last ten years, and was once again a newbie, heart-racing nervous at the mere thought of my first official interview.

Georg Han lives in a large house in a quiet, lovely neighborhood. This type of community belongs to another age, or so it seems to me, having spent most of my life in the shadows cast by downtown Toronto's monoliths of concrete, steel, and glass. People are watering their lawns and washing their cars; kids are bicycle-racing down the narrow streets; on the front porch of their home, an elderly couple is sitting hand-in-hand. I watch these moving images in the moving frame of my cab's backseat window, and I think that the last straw would be to see long-maned Golden Retrievers soaring through the air to catch frisbees in their teeth.

The cab pulls into the long, half-moon driveway. Someone is hunched over a garden of red flowers near the front of the house. As the cab approaches, she looks up. I pay the driver and step out of the car.

"Hello," she says, removing her gardening glove to shake my hand. She is twenty years my senior—late fifties or early sixties—and she is a beautiful woman. Her hair is gray and thinning, and her face is wrinkled, but there is beauty in the joy in her eyes and in her warm, welcoming smile, a beauty that no amount of years can hide.

Her name is Leslie Han, George Han's wife. She was surprised that I called—no one has shown professional interest in Han for years. He will be delighted to see you, she says. I'm not so sure, but I keep the thought to myself, graciously granting the possibility that she knows her husband better than I do.

What do I expect to find? A bitter, brooding has-been, angry at the world and anxious to take out his pent-up fury at the first reckless reporter who dared to disturb his social slumber?

What do I find instead, as Leslie leads me around the house to the backyard where George Han is swimming? Han is not a young man, but it seems no one has told him that he's old now.

He climbs out of the pool, almost launching himself through the rails at the final step. Leslie giggles and gives him a kiss as she hands him a towel. He wraps it around his body; skin hangs from him like a too-large suit might hang off of a prep school boy. But there is muscle beneath the skin—not only the memory of an athletic body, but the athletic body itself, if a little hidden.

His hair is grayer than Leslie's but thicker, and there is a familiar happiness in his brown eyes, as if he and Leslie have grown it together, along with the perennials in their garden.

A large weeping willow is protecting the lakeside edge of the backyard; it is within its shade, on Muskoka chairs, that George Han and I share a few beers ("There's nothing like a good, cold beer on a hot July day," he says) and talk, our every word captured by the faithful ears of my smartphone's microphone.

At first, it seems our roles are reversed; he asks if I've read any of his work, which I find hilarious and tell him so. He says that for years, he was interviewed by reporters who hadn't read anything he'd written. I tell him I've read *everything* he's written.

As I imagine is true of most writers, Han is a great listener. I tell him about the first time I read *Barefoot in the Snow*. I tell him that it was in reading his books that I first had the notion that I wanted to be a writer too; he says that's the greatest compliment one can pay a writer. He says that, among other things, writers are virus-carriers, and great writers infect others with their disease. I laugh at this curious metaphor, but Han just smiles.

He asks me if I've written anything. For a moment, I toy with the idea of lying, but the moment passes.

"A novel," I say, a little quietly.

"Is it any good?"

"I'm still working on it." I'm feeling uncomfortable; not too many people know that I've written a novel, and no one in the world has read it. "It's not really ready for publication or anything."

Han nods with a knowing smile.

Perhaps a little vindictively, I ask him why he stopped writing.

The question doesn't phase him; perhaps he's been expecting it. Before he answers, he shrugs, as if to say that anything that follows is a mere approximation, that his reasons can't be expressed in words alone.

"I used to love telling stories," Han says. "To my friends at school, to my little brother, to pretty girls. One day I realized that I could write down my stories instead of just telling them, and that's how I became a writer. Except that it wasn't good enough for most people. 'Are you published?' they asked. Well, no, I wasn't. So I set about getting published. But when I was published, they said, 'Well, sure, you've written and published short stories—anyone can do that. But can you write an entire novel?' So I wrote one, an entire novel. '*Writing* a novel is the easiest part,' they said. 'Just try getting it published.' So I tried, and got it published. 'How many awards has it won? Look around in a bookstore—just at the new releases. Anyone can get a novel published, it's winning awards that sets you apart.'"

"But it's still not good enough, right?" I say. "Even when you win the awards."

"That's right," Han says, smiling although I can see behind the smile a hint of the unresolved anger at these detracting voices from his past. "How many weeks was it on the bestseller list? Did Hollywood come calling? How many figures?"

"That's what you meant by chasing carrots."

Han nods. "They give you one carrot only to dangle another in front of you.

"You asked why I stopped publishing," he continues, which is not what I'd asked. "Every time I sat down at my keyboard, I saw those carrots hanging in front of me. 'This story won't win any awards,' I'd think. 'This one doesn't have Hollywood appeal.' I became paralyzed as a writer."

"So you cut the strings on the carrots," I say, as understanding dawns.

"No," Han says. "I threw off the riders."

"But you never quit writing."

Han smiles. "Next question."

I ask him the rest of my prepared questions, a little mechanically. Most of my mind is preoccupied with the crashing-wave of a thought: *He's been writing all along.* If the devil appears, I say to myself, and offers me the manuscripts in exchange for my soul, I may just strike the deal and consider him the sucker.

We've gone through four bottles of Moosehead between the two of us when Han asks if I'd like to see his study. One of my greatest pleasures in visiting people's homes is to stand in front of their shelves, to glance through the books they've accumulated, the books they bought or were given, and thought enough of to keep and display. "The books a person cherishes tell a story about that person"—the thought comes to me as a quote, but I can't place it.

"Yes," I say. "I'd like that very much."

Han's study is a large room on the top floor of his house. It is a book-lover's heaven: three giant bookshelves cover the walls, each shelf packed with all kinds of books: spine-cracked paperbacks; shiny-jacketed and jacketless hardcovers; tall, glossy trade editions. It is a mini library, with each book hand-picked by a single librarian. The fourth wall—the smallest one, interrupted as it is by a doorway—is completely bare. In front of it sits a small-monitored computer on an unassuming desk. I stare at this barren corner of the room and marvel that the stories Han wrote were perhaps first told to this small, ancient-looking computer and to the white wall behind it.

On Han's bookshelves, I count sixteen different copies of *Don Quixote* before I lose interest. Han says that he is like the Mel Gibson character in *Conspiracy Theory*, who can't come across a copy of *The Catcher in the Rye* and not buy it.

"I don't have many addictions," Han says. "But reading *Don Quixote* is one, and buying different copies of the book is another."

My goal of counting the copies of Cervantes's masterpiece was made harder by the fact that the different editions are not grouped together but scattered throughout. That is the most striking aspect of Han's collection: its unselfconscious hodepodgery.

Plato's *The Republic* kisses Heinlein's *The Puppet Masters*, which is next to a massive book with a fiery lion on its dark spine, an omnibus of Lewis's *The Chronicles of Narnia*. Dick's *The Three Stigmata of Palmer Eldritch* stands next to à Kempis's *The Imitation of Christ*, which leans into Coelho's *The Fifth Mountain*. A book of quotable notables is tall between two paperbacks, Dostoevsky's *Crime and Punishment* and an annotated copy of Shakespeare's *The Winter's Tale*. My finger continues running across the spines—the Bible; an anthology of the best short stories of the twentieth century; Sagan's *Cosmos*; Irving's *The World According to Garp*; Saint-Exupéry's *Le Petit Prince*; a three-volumes-in-one omnibus, Asimov's *Understanding Physics*; Chesterton's *The Ev-*

erlasting Man; an illustrated coffee table book of Coleridge's *The Rime of the Ancient Mariner*; Brontë's *Wuthering Heights* (I can't help but cry out, faux-melodramatically, "Heathcliff!" whenever I see that book); Homer's *The Odyssey*; a thick book collecting the 100 greatest poems written in English; Richler's *Barney's Version*; Gaarder's *Sophie's World*; Shelley's *Frankenstein*; Aristotle's *Ethics*; a book of Greek mythology; Lewis's *The Screwtape Letters*.

Books from humanity's ancient past sit alongside new releases; recognized classics of literature shoulder the most commercial of fiction. On Han's bookshelves, boundaries don't exist: science intermingles with fiction, biographies with mathematical puzzle books, graduate philosophy textbooks with cartoon-strip compendiums. Dispersed among the books are Han's own novels, in different editions and translations. It is as if he gives no more credit—but no less credit, either—to his own work.

"I'll admit to another addiction," Han says. "I can't resist a great story. It can be about how a giant metal cylinder that weighs tens of thousands of kilograms can get and stay airborne, or about Robin Hood rescuing Maid Marian. If it's an interesting story told in an interesting way, I'm your most attentive listener."

It seems almost redundant to ask him the darling question of author-interviewers. Who are his favorite writers? What are his influences? There they are, on the shelves. Maybe this is why he brought me to his study, so I wouldn't have to ask the question, or so he wouldn't have to enumerate them in his answer and risk missing a few.

As I've been looking through his collection, Han has kept his distance, watching me from afar. But unable to resist the siren song of his own books, he approaches and picks one from the shelf. It is Dickens's *A Christmas Carol*.

"Here is a perfect story," he says. "There is not a scene misplaced; and in all the tens of thousands of words, not a single one is a misstep. It is as perfect a work of fiction as there ever was and perhaps ever will be."

He closes his eyes and smells the book. If I hadn't done the same thing a thousand times with my own books, I might've found this custom quite strange. He replaces the book, picks another; they're transporting him, to the last time he read them, or perhaps the first time.

Emboldened by Han's actions, I pull out a book of my own— Goldman's *The Princess Bride*. I flip through it, allowing my gaze to fall on random passages, picking up sentences and paragraphs as I glide over the pages. I replace the book and pick up Joyce's *A Portrait of the Artist as a Young Man*.

It is almost a half-hour later when I notice that Han is looking at me.

"You asked if I stopped writing," Han says, when he sees he has my attention.

I nod.

"I didn't." The book he'd been holding—a slim paperback with yellowed pages—now rests on his lap.

"A novel?"

He nods and holds up his right hand, showing two fingers.

"*Two* novels? Can I read them?" The words are out before I can stop myself. "I—sorry, I—"

Han nods. He *nods*. As in: yes, you may read my books. "If I can read yours," he says.

Several hours, and a great dinner later, I leave him and his beautiful wife in their beautiful home.

Back in Toronto, I email him my book and he emails me both of his. I read them that night, one after the other; it is not the first time great books have kept me from sleeping. I call him the next day. "These need to be published. It's a crime not to publish them."

Han laughs. "Your book ain't so bad either."

As we'd exchanged books, we now exchange promises to publish our work.

"I guess we'll both be chasing carrots for a while," I say to Han on the phone.

"Try to keep that stuff in its place," he says, and I'm not sure if Han is speaking to me or to himself. "Try to remember that it's the work that matters, not the awards or the numbers, or the lack thereof. Books that bomb today may soar tomorrow."

"You're not worried, are you?" It's still odd to hear George Han speak as if he's merely mortal.

Han says that the world has grown cold toward his books in recent years.

"Not everyone in the world," I remind him.

There is a slightly awkward pause between us. Eventually, I thank him, perhaps for the thousandth time, for allowing me to interview him and for letting me read his books. I remind him once again of his promise to share them with the rest of the world. A world that's going to need a lot more carrots.

AFTERWORD

In the Gospels, Christ says a number of very scary things. One of the most frightening to me is His parable of the talents. The story according to St. Matthew goes like this: a rich man is departing for a long journey. He summons three servants and divides his money among them: five talents (a large sum) to the first, two to the second, and one to the third. Each servant has received the amount the master feels they can handle. When he returns, the master is happy to find that the first and second servants have doubled the money entrusted to them. The third servant however, motivated by fear, has done nothing with his talent but bury it in the ground to keep it safe. It turns out the servant's concerns were justified, although his strategy a gross miscalculation; the master's full fury is unleashed on this "lazy, evil, worthless" servant.

The parable wasn't on my mind when I decided I wanted to be a professional writer at the age of 15. I came up with an idea I thought was pretty good, wrote and edited the story, and sent it for review to the top magazine of speculative fiction at the time. The rejection I received a few weeks later knocked me off my feet; I'd never really failed at anything before, so this was a new, unexpected, and unpleasant feeling. But I picked myself up, dusted myself off, wrote another story and sent it in with renewed optimism and confidence. The rejection I received a few weeks later—well, I was now aware that rejection and failure were a possibility, so I was disappointed but not as shocked as the first time. It would take another 26 rejections over the next 3 years before I made my first sale ("They Came From Ooter's Place," collected in Part III of this book).

In some ways, that first bit of success is worse than continued failure. I'd sold my first story, which is what I'd been waiting for and what I felt would establish the path to a career as a writer, but many more rejections were to come between then and my next sale. And the sales themselves? Pretty paltry sums for the most part, especially in the early days.

The temptation to give up was always present. Writing is a lot of hard work and demands a great deal of your time. Unless you're independently wealthy, you need a day job to pay your bills, and that means you have to sacrifice other activities to find the time to write. Sometimes it's easily sacrificed things like watching TV, often it's necessary things like sleeping and eating, and—worst and hardest sacrifice of all—too often it's spending quality time with people that you love.

The parable was not on my mind when I wrote that first story, or even the next dozen. But from a place deep within my soul, it was Christ's parable that rebuked me whenever I thought that the return wasn't really worth my investment of time and effort. And it was Christ's parable that pulled me back onto the right track when I started to drift off course; it isn't just about using your talents, but using them in a certain way and for a certain purpose ("The Talent," in Part II of this book, is about just this idea). At some point, I managed to relax as a writer, and although "Chasing Carrots" is about many things (fear of failure and rejection, faith in one's abilities, love of books and of reading, to name a few), to me it's mostly about reaching the point (so natural at first, so hard to re-capture after you've made a few sales and received a few reviews) where you can write without too much self-consciousness; where you can write what you feel is important to write, without concern for fame or fortune.

Even if I've only been given a single talent's worth of talent (if you know what I mean), I believe I must do with it as much as I can before that day when the voice that spoke the world into existence says, "Tell me—what have you done with the talent I gave you?"

About the Author

Karl El-Koura was born in Dubai, United Arab Emirates in 1979 and currently lives in Ottawa, Ontario (Canada). He has published more than sixty short stories and articles. Karl holds a second-degree black belt in Okinawan Goju Ryu karate, is an avid commuter-cyclist, and works for the Canadian Federal Public Service.

Karl maintains an online home at http://www.ootersplace.com, where you can discover more work by him and keep up-to-date with his latest news. He can be reached at karl@ootersplace.com.

www.ingramcontent.com/pod-product-compliance
Lightning Source LLC
Chambersburg PA
CBHW020247150626
46552CB00020B/619